THE
MASADA
PROPOSAL

DAVID ORLO

TELLING STORIES THAT MATTER

Fluency Organization, Inc.
Design by Lindsay Taylor

THE
MASADA
PROPOSAL

DAVID ORLO

Fluency Organization, Inc.
Design by Lindsay Taylor

CAST OF CHARACTERS

**From *The Cloud Strike Prophecy* and
The Jerusalem Protocol:**

Tyler "Ty" Kensington – Former U.S. Marine
pilot and part-time contract *Mossad* agent

Regan Hart – Investment advisor, Global Wealth
Advisors

Solomon "Solly" Rubin – *Mossad* agent and
archeological tour guide in Israel

Asher Hazzan – Director, Israeli *Mossad*

Natan Abrams – Israeli Prime Minister

Ziv Kessler – Civilian businessman, trusted
advisor to Prime Minister Abrams

Abu Bakr al-Bagahdi – "The Fox," ISIS leader

New Characters:

Prologue, First Century Masada

Imma – Servant in the Jewish household of Yair
ben Tobias

Yair ben Tobias – Respected Jewish leader living in Jerusalem during the siege of the city

Bina – Wife of Yair

Mona – Adopted grandmother to Eleazar and Imma

Eleazar ben Yair – Oldest son of Yair, leader of the Jews living on Masada

Judah ben Yair – Youngest son of Yair

Lucius Flavius Silva – Roman governor of Judea and commanding general during the siege of Masada

King Herod – Ruler of the Jews who built the fortress of Masada

Iranian

Savyid Ali Mazdaki – Grand Ayatollah of the Islamic Republic of Iran

Turin Abassi – President of Iran

Dr. Parsa Turan – Iranian nuclear physicist in charge of uranium enrichment program

Etta Turan – Wife of Parsa

Ahmed Turan – Nine-year-old son of Parsa

Armeen Turan – Older brother of Parsa Armeen, respected physician in Tehran

Russian

Michael Sokolov – President of Russia

Benjamin Yukavits – Russian Prime Minister
General Sergey Novakova – Russian Minister
of Defense

Israeli
Eitan Barr – Chief Strategist, Operation Entebbe
Yoni Abrams – Commander, Operation Entebbe,
older brother of Prime Minister Natan Abrams
Professor Ehud Silverman – *Mossad's* foremost
expert on Islamic eschatology, professor at
Hebrew University, Jerusalem
Simon, Nikki, Daniel Guttenheim –
Residents of Qiryat Shemona
Avihay Stern – Mayor of Qiryat Shemona
Sven Johannessen – Swedish Olympic medalist,
Israeli citizen, and *Mossad* information officer

American
David Turner – President of the United States
Dr. Thomas Wagner – NASA scientist
Stephen Baker – CIA Director, Turner
administration
Tyson Alvarez – Chief of Staff, Turner
administration
Captain Curtis Morris – Commanding Officer
of the USS *George H.W. Bush*

"Today, we can point only to the fact that Masada has become a symbol of heroism and of Liberty for the Jewish people to whom it says: Fight to death rather than surrender; prefer death to bondage and loss of freedom."
Moshe Dayan, 1983

Dedicated in memory of
Bill McKenzie
Founder of Pine Cove Camps
Friend and fellow pilot
Constant encourager
CAVU for eternity!

PROLOGUE

73 A.D.

Imma awoke from a nightmare with a start and struggled with a moment of disorientation. "Where am I? What happened?" she mumbled. Then she remembered and stifled a scream. She yearned for the blessed darkness of sleep to return—forever, so she would not have to face the inevitable point of no return awaiting her.

A thin beam of sunlight crawled through a crack in a wooden door positioned two hundred steps above an underground water cistern where Imma had hidden on a small ridge of earth during the night.

Blinking as she glanced around at her surroundings, Imma saw the outline of her elderly adopted grandmother, Mona, still asleep beside her. Five young orphans who were in their care huddled next to Mona. *"Good,"* Imma thought. They were still in the blessed place of their dreams. She wondered if they were having the same nightmares she'd had.

As her eyes slowly adjusted to her eerie, black surroundings, she heard a few water droplets ping the surface of the water, echoing in the massive chamber. Imma wrapped her arms around her knees to keep from shivering—from the chilly air and dreadful memories of the previous evening.

Still, she closed her eyes and willed herself to go back there in her mind.

After all, it was now her job to remember. Everything.

Imma was the one chosen by her master, Eleazar ben Yair, to live to tell the story. He'd selected her for this responsibility because of her skills since she could read and write in several languages, a rare talent for any slave, much less a female. Through a strange twist of fate, Imma had learned Latin, Greek, and Aramaic as a teenager. She spoke each language fluently and possessed an amazing ability to recall details.

Now, as she hid from her enemies in the bosom of the earth, Imma took a deep breath and realized she would be discovered soon by her enemies. She would need to recall the facts of the story as if they were written down on parchment in her mind.

Seven Years Earlier
66 A.D.

Imma had been living happily in Jerusalem for ten years as a servant in the household of a wealthy Jew named Yair ben Tobias. Although a slave, she was treated with a kindness reserved for family members.

Imma had been born sixteen years earlier in Athens, where her family abandoned her for reasons unknown. Entirely on her own with nowhere to go, it was not long before the Roman army captured her as a slave. A wealthy Roman Centurion named Crispus bought her on auction and assigned her the mundane household tasks of a servant in Greece.

Even though she had never learned as a child to read or write, Imma was a quick learner and soon learned to speak in Latin to the other servants in Crispus' household. She was also maturing into a beautiful teenager, with flawless bronze skin and a brilliant smile. Her thick, black hair was her most notable feature, although she kept it tied back in a braid when she was working.

When the Romans later assigned Crispus to the remote outpost of Jerusalem, he brought Imma with him. There Crispus developed a mutually respectful friendship with Yair ben Tobias, a leading member of the Sadducees, a powerful religious Jewish ruling party of the time. Sadducees were often friends of Romans and readily adopted Roman customs and dress. Not every Jew took to the Romans this way, however, especially not a man like Yair ben Tobias. Yair needed a servant to provide care for his sons, so Cripus agreed to sell Imma to him for fifty denarii before he left for yet another new assignment.

Fate changed Imma's life when Bina, the wife of Yair, grew to love the young girl as the daughter she never had. Bina lived up to her name, "intelligence and wisdom," teaching Imma to speak Aramaic and to read and write her native Greek language. Bina was amazed at how quickly Imma learned. She also instructed Imma in their Jewish faith and the one true God who existed far above any idols made by human hands.

Imma's primary job involved tutoring Bina's two sons: Eleazar, the older, and Judah, the younger. They were robust and charming, and she felt as close to them as members of her own family. Likewise, the two boys treated her like an older sister.

When three years passed, the political and economic situation in Jerusalem had turned dangerous because of an increasing movement to rebel against the occupying Roman army. By 66 A.D., the situation had become so unsafe that it was hazardous for people to walk alone at night.

Over the strong objections of their father, Eleazar and Judah joined a group of zealots whose fanatical hatred against Romans had infected the entire city. Yair's household was now divided, a common curse among families of that day who could not see eye to eye on the dueling political issues at hand.

The young men in these rebellious bands carried out nighttime attacks against Roman sentries, even marauding Jews like Yair who appeared to be too sympathetic to the Romans. The Romans called them the Sicarii after the small but effective daggers the attackers concealed under their robes. As time went on, the young men became more brazen and indiscriminate. One day Yair's brother, Menahem, was murdered by one of the factions of zealots for his vocal support of the Romans.

Yair was heartbroken and begged his boys not to risk being a part of a group that was destined to catch the attention of the Roman army for their misdeeds. But they refused.

The Roman general Titus finally had enough and responded to the Jewish rebellion with harsh measures. He rounded up zealots by the hundreds and crucified them on every tree surrounding the city. As an extra precaution, he then enforced an embargo, preventing any food or supplies from entering Jerusalem. The citizens would slowly starve.

It was then that Yair realized that he must get
his family out of the city for their safety. When the
residents of Jerusalem were nearly out of food, some
became so deranged that they were tempted to eat
their own children.

He knew of the irrepressible might of the Roman
army and sent word by messenger to Crispus to
arrange a private meeting. He asked his friend to
escort his family safely out of Jerusalem, offering him
almost all of his meager wealth to help them escape.

Eleazar hated his father for striking a deal,
although he had to admit the indisputable wisdom
in leaving a city on the cusp of madness and ruin.
Eventually, Eleazar agreed to flee Jerusalem with his
father, but only so that he could continue to organize
the fight outside the city. Judah, however, refused to
leave at any cost. Eleazar would never see his brother
again.

Under cover of darkness one night, a group of
soldiers under Crispus' command smuggled Yair, Bina,
Eleazar, and Imma out. The Roman guard covered the
family of Jews in a burlap sheet on the back of a wagon,
disguising their bodies as corpses to be disposed of
outside the city. The horse-drawn procession climbed
the Mount of Olives east of Jerusalem without being
detected and started downhill toward the desert.

Once they were safely outside of Bethany, the

Roman escort brought the wagon to a halt. The commander's eyes were cold as he told the Jewish refugees that they were now on their own to walk the rest of their journey, carrying with them only a few necessities and some water.

Eleazar had received word that a Jewish community of refugees had formed nearby on former King Herod's abandoned fortress named Masada. The flat-topped mountain towered hundreds of feet above the Dead Sea and provided a natural plateau of safety for the rebels who had gathered there with their families to escape the Roman threat. Encouraged by this news, Yair and his family turned south and started the long journey seventy miles through the harsh desert to join their Jewish brothers on Masada, a place the family hoped would be their new home.

***

Despite their attempts to ration their provisions, they soon depleted their supply of food and water. Both Yair and Bina were already weak from months of malnutrition during the siege. They struggled to climb up and down the tall desert mountains in the searing heat and soon succumbed to the relentless sun and unyielding thirst.

Imma and Eleazar dug shallow graves and covered their loved ones' bodies with stones. Despite their youthfulness, they would have perished themselves had they not made it to the springs of *Ein Gedi* the next day. They found precious water there in the crags of the mountains and met up with a handful of other Jewish refugees who were also traveling to Masada.

The travelers told Eleazar and Imma some amazing news. They had heard that almost one thousand Jews were now rallying on top of Masada, and more were joining them every week. Eleazar and Imma set out the next morning to reach Masada, but they could not help but wonder what conditions would prevail on top of the mountain among a thousand desperate and starving people. After climbing the steep Snake Trail that wound up the side of the natural outcropping of earth, they were surprised by what they found. The refugees were not suffering but rather enjoying an unexpected surplus of food and water, thanks to the ingenuity of Masada's original designer, King Herod.

When Herod had built his remarkable fortress almost a hundred years earlier, he had been paranoid about maintaining his safety at this remote royal residence. Although he planned to spend only the winters there, he built forty storehouses large enough to hold many years' supplies of non-perishable food and installed several barracks, armories, guest facilities, and even two swimming pools.

The ridge of the mountain was lined with a double

casement stone wall. Thirty-eight watchtowers sat along the perimeter to spot any approaching enemies. Masada housed two palaces—a western residence for guests and an opulent home for himself on the northern end. His personal home balanced precariously on the side of the cliff, offering wraparound views of the Jordan Valley.

Water was the most valuable resource in the desert, so Herod designed an ingenious system to sustain his entire fortress. In addition to supplying water to drink, the elaborate engineering allowed him to irrigate the rich soil and plant lush gardens yielding abundant quantities of fruit and vegetables—enough to live off of for many years.

At the heart of the innovative construction was a bi-level network of twelve cisterns carefully excavated out of solid stone around the base of the mountain. During the winter rains, water would collect here as it dripped down the sides of Masada. However, in this extraordinarily dry climate rainwater alone was not sufficient, but the rain in Judea often set off a surge of flashfloods draining toward the Dead Sea. He ordered his engineers and slaves to build a dam across one of the gorges to catch the water, which was then diverted through a system of aqueducts using the power of gravity to top off the plaster-covered cisterns at the western base of Masada.

The twelve cisterns were designed so that when one filled up, it would overflow into the next container. Then the water would be transferred to the top of Masada by a constant parade of donkeys that made their way up the winding Snake Trail to the summit. Each animal carried large pots of water that were emptied into two enormous underground cisterns on top of the fortress for everyday use.

After Herod's death, the stores of food remained, along with a near-permanent supply of water. For all his careful planning, Herod could not have foretold how this ingenuity would play into the riveting story of Masada.

***

Time passed slowly for the hundreds of Jewish families biding their time on Masada. Weeks turned into months, which then turned into years of interminable waiting.

Within the first year, Eleazar became the undisputed leader of the rebels. Over the next six years, he married and fathered two fine sons Judah and Menahem, named after his younger brother and uncle. Eleazar also provided food and shelter for five young orphans who were cared for by his adopted grandmother, Mona, who had no other family.

The close-knit members of this sizeable Jewish

community spent their time working the gardens and fortifying the walls around their homes atop Masada. Each family shared a foreboding sense that the Romans wouldn't ignore them indefinitely.

70 A.D.

One day the Jews on Masada saw a massive plume of smoke obscuring the sky to the northwest—the direction of their beloved Jerusalem. Before long, they could smell the pungent odor of an inferno that lasted many days.

A few weeks later, a breathless messenger arrived from Jerusalem. He described the shocking story of how the Romans had utterly destroyed the entire city. To their astonishment, they learned that the Romans had even razed the Holy Temple and plundered its treasures. Eleazar's gaze became dark as he listened to this news. With Jerusalem sacked, he knew that the emboldened Roman army would soon turn their attention to extinguishing the last band of Jewish resistance—all those gathered on Masada. It might be a year or more before the Romans came, he thought, but they were coming.

It was almost two years before the Roman governor of Judea and commanding general, Lucius

Flavius Silva, led the mighty Roman Tenth Legion to Masada after the destruction of Jerusalem in 70 A.D. As a humiliating show of force, the army brought with them thousands of Jewish prisoners of war captured from Jerusalem who became forced labor for the Romans.

Silva was a brilliant tactician, and after studying the situation on Masada, he decided the best course of action was to starve the Jewish rebels.

He ordered his soldiers and slaves to build eight camps around the base of the mountain fortress, each connected by a tall stone wall to cut off any means of escape for the Jews. His psychological warfare strategy issued a stern message: "Where I can put a stone, I can put a soldier."

The Romans then settled into their camps to wait, prepared for another long siege. But they miscalculated the ample provisions of the Jewish rebels. The Romans regularly brought in water and food to feed their army and Jewish slaves, but the rebels had enough provisions to last them forever it seemed. It would be two long years before the story was over. And it would not end in a way that anyone could predict.

While the Roman army below suffered from meager water rations, the rebels regularly responded with their own version of psychological warfare.

Eleazar ordered his soldiers to draw precious pots of water from their abundant cisterns and pour it over the sides of the mountains. The soldiers below who were fighting for every sip of water they could get saw that the Jews had water to waste and realized they would not be giving up anytime soon.

Silva soon concluded that he would never starve the rebels out of the well-supplied fortress. Instead, he decided to attack. Eleazar and his officers watched as a fleet of Roman engineers began building an ominous ramp on the western side of the mountain in preparation for a raid.

While constructing this massive ramp, the Roman and Jewish armies practiced dueling strategies to outwit the other for months on end. To slow the progress of the Romans, Eleazar first ordered his comrades to throw stones at the construction crew of soldiers. The Romans countered this move with a tortoise-like defense, joining shields above the heads of their fellow soldiers to deflect the rocks. That worked until the rebels started rolling huge boulders down the ramp, flattening anyone in their way.

Silva countered this new strategy by exchanging his Roman soldiers with Jewish slaves to finish the ramp. If the slaves refused to work, the guards tortured them in sight of their Jewish brothers above. The rebels faced a dilemma. Would they kill their own countrymen—some of whom they knew—or allow the ramp to be built?

Eleazar was a principled man, and Imma was not surprised when he decided he could not kill his Jewish brothers. To the Jews' dismay, the Roman ramp grew higher with each passing day.

Imma recalled how the rebels' anxiety grew in proportion to the advance of the project. They were trapped. The discussion at every meal and gathering centered on one thing: how soon the Romans would reach the top of the mountain. There were many opinions about how to defend themselves, but all the ideas sounded futile in the end. The leaders of each opposing army expected a violent confrontation to happen—sooner rather than later.

In the meantime, Eleazar worked quickly to fortify the walls where the ramp would inevitably reach the side of the cliff. For weeks his men moved massive wooden timbers to reinforce the double stone walls. They piled stones and wedged sand between the walls so that any pressure applied from the outside would compact the fill dirt. These efforts were their only hope, but Eleazar still feared they would prove ineffective against the sheer might and number of the Romans.

As the sinister slope neared the top, the Romans changed tactics once more. They instructed the already exhausted band of Jewish slaves to construct a tall, ironclad siege tower housing a gigantic battering ram. The structure lay on its side during its construction until pulleys raised it to its full height in front of the rebels' gate.

Eleazar and his sons watched in horror as catapults mounted on the siege tower then hurled fiery projectiles over the walls onto the camp of the desperate rebels, sending screaming women and children running for shelter as men called for water to extinguish the flames.

In the heat of the fierce battle, the wind shifted, and fire engulfed the Roman tower. A cheer of victory arose from the rebels with this twist of fate. But the reprieve was only momentary because the wind changed again and began to consume the rebel camp. As the Jews sought cover from the advancing Romans charging up the ramp, the enormous battering ram crushed the stone walls to rubble. Eleazar concluded that the Roman soldiers would take the entire mountain in only a few hours.

But the sun was setting, and Roman armies never fought in darkness. Instead, Silva retreated and set guards at the gate alongside a group of Jewish slaves. He sent the remaining soldiers back down to their camps for the night and planned to attack in the light of the next day. Remembering the many taunts and casualties inflicted on the Romans, Silva relished an act of slow, agonizing revenge on these Jewish agitators.

That night, Eleazar made plans of his own and called together his sons, Judah and Menahem, along with all the other families. The solemn assembly gathered in the open area surrounding the small synagogue. After prayers led by the high priest, Jonathan, Eleazar moved to address the weary and despondent crowd.

Imma recalled the expressions of shock and horror in the faces of the people she had come to know and love over the years. Women and children wept openly, and the men stood defiantly with their weapons ready. They might die, they assured each other, but they would take as many Romans with them as possible. Some of the men even insisted that they attack the Romans during the night.

Eleazar called for silence and began to speak.

He had already calculated what cruelty the Romans would exact on the men, women, and children in just a few hours. He had come to offer his people an unexpected solution. The Masada Proposal, as it came to be known, was recorded in history and would be discussed and debated for many centuries.

He began, "Since we long ago, my generous friends, resolved never to be servants to the Romans nor to any other than to God himself, who alone is the true and just Lord of mankind, this time is now come that obliges us to make that resolution true in practice."

There was a murmur from the audience as they pondered what he meant. What choice did they have in this hopeless matter?

Eleazar continued, "We are the very first that revolted from the enemy, and we are the last that fight against them. And I cannot but esteem it as a favor that God has granted us, that it is still in our power to die bravely and in a state of freedom. It is very plain that we shall be taken within a day's time; but it is still an eligible thing to die, after a glorious manner, together with our dearest friends."

At this suggestion, there was a muted roar of displeasure. They instinctively refused to consider what Eleazar was suggesting. Surely he did not want them to die. Or did he? He waved his hand for silence and continued.

"As for all our brothers who have died in this war against the Romans, it is reasonable that we should esteem them blessed, for they are dead in defending, and not in betraying their liberty. But as to our brothers who are now under the Romans, who would not pity their condition? Some of them have been put upon the rack and tortured with fire and whippings, and so died. Some have been half-devoured by wild beasts and yet have been reserved alive to be devoured by them a second time, in order to afford laughter and sport to our enemies."

The sound of drunken laughter and singing drifted up from the Roman camps below at that very moment. The irony only punctuated the truth of Eleazar's words. He pointed his finger northwestward and shouted, "And where is now that great city, the metropolis of the Jewish nation? Where is this city that was believed to have God himself inhabiting therein? It is now demolished to the very foundations."

Eleazar slashed his fist down into his palm. "And," he yelled, "the only monument of it preserved is the vile camp of those who destroyed it that dwells upon its ruins!" With this, he cast a glance below at the Roman soldiers and took a pause. His voice grew soft. "I cannot but wish that we had all died before we had seen that holy city demolished by the hands of our enemies, or the foundations of our holy temple dug up after so profane a manner."

At the mention of the holy temple, the Jews began wailing uncontrollably. Many of the women fell to their knees and groaned in grief over the holy city of God.

Eleazar spoke the next words with measured cadence. "But since we had a glorious hope that deluded us, perhaps we might now be able to avenge ourselves on our enemies on that account."

The men looked at one another in confusion—how could they avenge themselves on an enemy poised to destroy them at first light?

Eleazar explained, "Let us make haste to die bravely. Let us pity to ourselves, our children, and our wives, while it is in our own power to show pity to them. For we were born to die; nor is it in the power of the most happy of our race to avoid it. But for abuses and slavery, and the sight of our wives led away after an ignominious manner, with their children, these are not such evils as are natural and necessary among men."

He looked intently at his friends and neighbors, pleading with them to understand and agree with his proposal to save their dignity. "Who will not, therefore, believe that the Romans will certainly be in a rage against us if they take us alive?"

The Jews nodded in agreement. It would be a fate too terrible to consider.

Eleazar painted the picture of what fate awaited them if they did nothing. He did not want anyone to misunderstand the inevitability of their suffering. "Miserable will be the young men who will be strong enough in their bodies to sustain many torments," he said. "Miserable will be those of elder years, who will not be able to bear those same calamities. One man will be obliged to hear the voice of his son implore the help of his father when his hands are bound."

This very scene would undoubtedly play out over and over in a matter of hours. And every family knew it.

Eleazar argued once more, "But certainly, our hands are still at liberty, and we have a sword in them. Let us die before we become slaves under our enemies. Let us go out of the world together with our children and our wives in a state of freedom. This is what our laws command us to do. That is what our wives and children crave at our hands."

At this point, the men started to bang their weapons together, making a great noise that threatened to drown out Eleazar's words.

"No," he continued, "God himself has brought this necessity among us. The Romans desire to enslave us. Let us, therefore, make haste and instead of affording them such pleasure, let us leave them an example which shall at once cause their astonishment at our death and their admiration of our hardiness therein."

There could be no mistaking now what Eleazar suggested: take their life and liberty into their own hands that night—instead of being taken by force by morning.

Imma and Mona huddled beside the synagogue

with the five young orphans surrounding them as they observed what was happening. Mona looked at Imma for consolation. Was this really happening? What was going on? Was everyone going to die this night?

A surreal scene began to play out before their eyes. Without a word, husbands embraced their wives and children, knowing it would be the last time they would do so on earth. They took their loved ones in their arms and gave them parting kisses as they wept bitterly with their families. Then each husband dutifully, but tenderly used his sword to take the life of his wife and children.

Imma and Mona covered the orphans' eyes and turned their backs, unable to stomach the bloodshed of their friends and fellow Jews. They held their hands to their ears, but nothing could muffle the mournful wails all around them. The two women were also crying, realizing that it would be their turn to die in the next few moments.

Suddenly Eleazar placed his hand on Imma's shoulder. She turned to see the agonized look in his eyes. She expected death to come quickly. Eleazar bent near her neck and she relaxed, wondering how long she would feel the warmth of her blood trickling down her skin before she passed out. Instead of being afraid, a strange sense of peace washed over her.

"Let it come," she thought. She was ready.

Then Eleazar's voice cut through the night air. "Imma, I want you to take Mona and the children down into the large cistern. The Romans may spare your lives. If they allow you to live, there must be someone to tell our story. I'm counting on you to do that."

Dazed, Imma could only nod her head as Eleazar helped her and Mona to their feet. The children quietly followed them to the large cistern nearby. He opened a wooden door and led them down the steep steps into the depths of the earth.

Eleazar said, "Stay here for the night. You will be well hidden. We can only hope and pray that the Romans will spare you."

The orphans were all crying, and Eleazar hugged each one while looking deep into their eyes. "Make me proud, children," he said. "Never forget what happened here."

He embraced Mona a final time and smoothed her gray hair, soothing her with his voice. "Thank you, Grandmother, for sharing your life and your family with us. Take care of these children."

He turned to Imma, who was trying to catch her breath. A mixture of fear and grief had reduced her to speechless tears. Eleazar took her hand and said, "Imma, you have been family to me. I love you as my dear sister. You must be the brave one after me.

You must live to tell the story of the courage of these families who chose death over slavery."

Then he turned to climb up the long stairway leading out of the cistern, closing the door behind him. He noticed a dark silence, a quiet that had not fallen on Masada since the first rebels had arrived. The wives and children of his friends and comrades who had been busily working earlier that day now lay sleeping in the peace of death. Over one hundred remaining men stood still, swords clenched by their side, their clothes stained with the blood of their families.

Eleazar summoned the survivors to him. To a Jew, suicide was the most hideous of all sins, and none could envision taking their own lives. Therefore, Eleazar had the remaining fathers draw lots. The men took their time taking small pieces of tile from a basket. All of the tiles were black, except for ten white tiles. One unique white tile bore the Hebrew letters *chet* and *yud*, meaning "life."

He explained, "Those ten of you who chose the white tiles will send all of us to sleep beside our families. One of you will then take the lives of his nine remaining brothers. Who has the tile with the letters?"

A young father named Benjamin stepped forward, holding up the ivory tile with the special designation.

"I have it," he said with a choked voice.

Eleazar placed his hand on the young man's shoulder and said, "Thank you, brother Benjamin. You have been chosen for an important task. You will show mercy to your fellow soldiers by sending them to be with their families in the afterlife. Once you have done so, it will be your duty to fall on your sword. By your merciful willingness, may the God of our Fathers grant you life in the hereafter. Today is the fifteenth day of Nissan. Today is the day of the Passover sacrifice. May God honor your sacrifice."

Eleazar turned to the handful of men who would be slaying the others. "My only request is that before you sleep in death, set fire to all the possessions and treasure of our community. But leave the food and water stores. I want our enemy to see all our provisions. I want them to realize that we could have survived for much longer."

Eleazar nodded his head to signal he was finished talking.

***

That night had been so terrible. So unbelievable.

Imma spent the rest of the evening in the cistern trying to remember as much of Eleazar's speech as possible. She repeated sections to herself for hours, vowing to commit them to paper if she survived and was allowed quill and parchment.

By morning, Imma wondered if she'd dreamed all that she now recalled. Suddenly the sound of Roman soldiers shouting orders to each other interrupted her thoughts. Mona and the children awoke, and Imma gestured for them to keep silent. Perhaps the Romans would leave, and they could make their escape.

But after an hour of waiting, the door leading to the stairs to the cistern flew open, sending sunlight streaming into the darkness. The light briefly blinded them.

Imma met eyes with a young Roman soldier seconds before he turned his head and shouted to his commanding officer, "I have found some people alive! Come quickly!"

Several soldiers then tumbled down the steps, and their rough hands dragged the limp band of survivors up to the surface of the mountain fortress. Imma saw the morbid outlines of almost a thousand bodies lying in perfect order beside each other. Except for the sporadic calls of the soldiers looking for more survivors, an unnatural silence enveloped the mountain. No one, it seemed, could understand what had transpired during the night.

The guards took Imma, Mona, and the children directly to General Silva. His face contorted in an expression of unbelief. He stared at Imma and asked, "Do you speak Greek?"

Imma didn't dare raise her eyes to his.

"I do, sir," she replied.

Silva waved his hand toward the bodies of the rebels and demanded, "Then in the name of the Emperor, can you tell me what happened here?"

Imma met his gaze and said, "Yes, sir. I will. Can you provide me with a quill, ink, and parchment?"

She expected to be tortured and perhaps killed. But while she still had life, she had to make sure the real story of Masada would never die.

***

Dawn

Eastern slope of Masada
May 14, 1986

As the Eastern sky leaked the first shafts of light, Natan Abrams leaned forward and continued to march. He was aware of the other members of his Israeli Defense Force squad advancing around him. The only sounds were the rhythmic crunch of the boots on the rocky soil and the labored breathing of the new IDF recruits.

His neck and back were ablaze with a throbbing soreness from carrying the forty-pound pack. It felt as if he had been marching for two days, but his brain reminded him that they left their camp a little over four hours earlier. He would pay all the shekels to his name if he could stop, rest, and drink from his canteen, but he kept going for the sake of his comrades. They had chosen him to serve at the front as squad leader, and he would never disappoint them.

Natan's fatigue mingled with a sense of anticipation. Today would be the graduation ceremony for *Tironut*, basic training in the Israeli army. Natan's eighteenth birthday party was only a dim memory now. After the past four months of intense physical, mental, and military training, he felt as if he had aged ten years.

Suddenly the early morning silence shattered as the First Sergeant yelled, "Company, halt!" Instantly, the men and women in the squad stopped. Dust from their trek continued the march in front of them, carried by the desert wind.

Natan glanced up at the rising shadow of the fortress of Masada. He had visited the site dozens of times and had even raced up the popular Snake Trail on the eastern side when he was just a young boy visiting from Tel Aviv. This time he would make that journey in full military gear.

As they continued in single file procession, Natan shivered at the abrupt thought of almost one thousand of his Jewish ancestors choosing death on this mountaintop over Roman slavery. At the same time he found himself possessing a deep-seated assurance that he would also be willing to die for the freedom that his people enjoyed. He understood now why the IDF brought thousands of recruits to Masada for their swearing in ceremony.

Finally, they arrived at the top of the mountain and assembled before the raised platform erected for the ceremony.

The men stood in silence, looking out over the edge of Masada and the endless stretch of desert, mountains, gorges, and valleys.

"Company, attention!" the tough platoon sergeant shouted. During his training Natan had not seen him smile once.

Natan stood with his backbone erect, his shoulders back and his chin down. The thrill of this moment chased away the demons of pain that had tormented him on the thirty-five-mile trek.

"Left face!" the commander said. "Repeat this oath after me."

The squad members shouted, "Yes, sir!"

"I swear and commit to maintain allegiance to the State of Israel...

Its laws, and its authorities...

To accept upon myself unconditionally...

The discipline of the Israel Defense Forces...
To obey all the orders and instructions...
Given by authorized commanders...
And to devote all my energies...
And even sacrifice my life...
For the protection of the homeland and the liberty of Israel.
This I swear."

Along with his fellow squad members, Natan shouted, "This I swear!" as loudly as he could.

Then, without any leading, the squad leaders began to chant the words that every group of new IDF soldiers vocalizes:

"Masada will never fall again!"
"Masada will never fall again!"
"Masada will never fall again!"

Natan roared his oath along with his fellow warriors. The sound became deafening as over and over they bellowed their promise. Then as their shouts died, echoes from the valleys surrounding Masada brought back the same words: "Masada will never fall again." To Natan, it was as if he heard the ghostly voice of his ancestors who had sacrificed themselves on this mountain.

It was a turning point in the life of Natan Abrams. However, he never imagined that one day he would become Prime Minister of Israel, and it would be up to him to see that this solemn promise he made on Masada as a young man would stand against overwhelming odds.

1

Jezzine, Southern Lebanon

Abu Bakr al-Bagahdi usually relished the cool evening breeze. But instead of invigorating him, tonight it chilled him. He stood alone, gazing up at the star-filled sky, trying in vain to resist the biting wind. The seething anger inside him was powerless to fight the cold. He wanted to break something—preferably the necks of those who had thwarted his vision for a Holy Caliphate.

He closed his eyes and spoke his frustration aloud. "I came within minutes of destroying the Israeli capital and wiping out millions of infidels. I would have claimed the entire Levant region for the glorious Caliphate for Allah! It was Allah's perfect plan."

But this plan had been ruined by cowards and idiots at the last minute. "It wasn't Inshallah," he reminded himself. "No, no. It was not God's will. It was human stupidity!"

He lowered his right hand and seized the hilt of his razor edged sword resting in the scabbard on his left hip. He slowly removed the deadly instrument and stared at the forged steel. Al-Bagahdi had wielded this sword dozens of times, chopping off the heads of both infidels and Islamic State soldiers who had betrayed him. He had even carefully staged many executions in front of high definition cameras to record the murders and upload the footage to hundreds of Islamic State social media platforms.

He swung the sword in a vicious arc through the night air and imagined the ecstasy of severing the head of Ahmad Karim, the ISIS videographer who had betrayed him.

"You traitor! I trusted you!" he shouted into the night. "But you were a pig-spy for the dirty Jews. You warned them of my glorious plan to destroy their pagan capital, Jerusalem. You have run away like the dog you are. But they don't call me the Fox for nothing. I swear by Allah that I will find you. And when I do, you will feel the sting of my sword!"

Al-Bagahdi spun and swung the sword again, facing yet another imaginary enemy. He screamed back into the darkness, "And you, Ali el-Gamal, you were my most trusted aid. I commanded you to deliver and detonate the nuclear device in the Old City of Jerusalem. But, being the coward you are, you gave the job to idiots while you fled like a frightened rat."

A wicked smile broke through al-Bagahdi's thick, black beard as he recalled seeing the satellite image of an Israeli missile slamming into el-Gamal's fleeing Mercedes. The car and occupants were incinerated in a matter of seconds.

"And you got what you deserved. I hope you are burning in the hottest fires of hell, Ali."

But it seemed as if the Islamic State was going to hell, too. Just two years earlier, the Islamic State had controlled roughly one-third of the territory around the border of Syria and Iraq. Raqqa had been their main base, but they quickly captured five major cities. His fighters had swept into Abu Ghrab, Falluja, Tikrit, and Manbij before they captured their largest city, Mosul. The Islamic State was on track to become a true Islamic nation after that. In each of these cities they had methodically imposed their radical Islamic standards. Christian men were beheaded, young women were taken as involuntary wives for the fighters, and even Muslims were subjected to the rigid rules of the Caliphate.

But now al-Bagahdi realized that this earlier conquest was just a distant memory. With the election of a new American president, the Caliphate had begun to crumble. President David Turner sent

U.S. Special Forces back into Iraq and was allowing the U.S. military leaders to fight the war as they saw fit.

Since then, the Islamic State had lost most of their grip on the vast area between Syria and Iraq. Recruiting numbers were down. U.S. cybersecurity experts had frozen their assets. Russian and U.S. jets and drones had bombed their oil production facilities into disuse.

The American-led Iraqi forces soon recaptured every city, including Mosul. Then they forced al-Bagahdi to flee from his base in Raqqa. Al-Bagahdi spat on the ground and moaned, "It's hard to establish a Caliphate without a country."

He knew that there was still hope for a renewed effort among his secret forces hidden away in Lebanon. His ISIL fighters had infiltrated the leadership of Hezbollah, and it had been a simple matter to move his base of operations to Jezzine, Lebanon. It was the perfect place to hide in plain sight. There were many Hezbollah strongholds in Lebanon, but they were all under constant surveillance. Jezzine was a small, mountaintop city filled with a majority of Marionite Christians. Nobody would think to look for ISIS or Hezbollah soldiers here. And the unsuspecting Christians in Jezzine had no idea that their days were numbered.

Whether his fighters were called ISIL, Daesh, or

Hezbollah mattered little to al-Bagahdi. He smiled and said to himself, *"They can call us the Boy Scouts if they like. As long as we see the growing pile of bloody corpses of Christians, Jews, and false Muslims, any title will do."*

Al-Bagahdi's cell phone began to vibrate in his vest. *"That's strange,"* he thought. It was a burner phone, and nobody knew he had it. He looked at the screen and it read, "Unknown Caller." He pushed a button to disconnect the call.

Before he could return the phone to his vest, it began buzzing again. He hesitated before thinking, *"If I answer and it is someone from the Coalition forces calling, they can pinpoint my location for a smart bomb."*

As the phone continued to vibrate, his curiosity won out. He punched the "talk" icon and yelled, "Speak!"

There was a moment of silence before a voice said in Arabic, "I believe I am speaking to the *mujahideen* who has been called the Fox."

Al-Bagahdi was still skeptical so he refused to take the bait. "I don't know anyone by the name of the Fox."

The caller chuckled, "We can dispense of nicknames for now. But I believe the two of us share a common mission."

"And what would this common mission be?"

The voice growled, "The total annihilation of

the occupying nation of Israel and the ultimate destruction of the Great Satan, the United States of America."

Al-Bagahdi's pulse quickened. "Who are you and just how do you plan to accomplish this mission?"

There was another pause before the voice said, "I am Savyid Ali Mazdaki, Grand Ayatollah of the Islamic Republic of Iran."

"I doubt it. And how did you get my number, by the way?"

"Oh, believe me, Mr. Al-Bagahdi, I am the Grand Ayatollah. VAJA, our Iranian Intelligence Service can pinpoint your hiding spot there in Southern Lebanon. Better us than the Coalition smart bombs, huh? Now, are you ready to destroy Israel and the U.S. for the glory of Islam?"

Al-Bagahdi lips curled through his thick black beard. "I'm listening."

2

Masada, Near the Judean Desert

As dawn arrived, the sky over the Jordanian hills east of the Dead Sea transformed into a mixed palate of dark blue and orange-pink. Three friends, Regan, Ty, and Solly, had started their arduous climb up the Snake Trail of Masada an hour earlier while the sky was still stained black and stippled with stars. As they arrived at the summit, they paused to catch their breath and admire the canvas of color to the east.

Regan Hart was slim, fit, and the youngest of the trio. As she wiped her brow, she tucked tendrils of her long, blonde hair back under her Harvard University cap. Receiving her MBA from Harvard seemed like a lifetime ago, but it was only seven years behind her. After graduation, she had helped create proprietary software that had revolutionized the investment industry. In her past, she had quickly climbed the corporate ladder at Global Wealth Advisors. But again, that portion of her life also seemed like decades ago. Her purchase of dozens of stocks at their IPOs produced a steady income from escalating dividends. To maintain her lifestyle, she kept a few of her favorite clients and could work anywhere in the world with access to the Internet.

Regan had met Ty Kensington by chance when someone had burglarized her apartment in Atlanta four years earlier. Ty was a former U.S. Marine pilot who was working as a private investigator at the time Regan was robbed. In his early 40s, Ty was still in great shape with wide shoulders and a trim waist stacked on his six-foot-two-inch frame. His dark hair was sprinkled with a dusting of gray.

There had been an immediate attraction between the two, but dangerous circumstances and similar dominant personalities had kept them at odds for most of their relationship.

The third member of the group was Solomon Rubin. "Solly," as he was known to his friends, was an Israeli who had immigrated from Australia in the mid-1970s. Solly was a jovial man with a quick laugh and a constant sparkle in his eyes. He sported a long, white beard. A braided ponytail meandered down his back under his trademark Stetson cowboy hat.

Solly was officially employed as an archeological

tour guide and had more knowledge about the ruins of Israel than most of the Ph.Ds employed by the Israeli Antiquities Authority. Unofficially, Solly had also worked undercover as a special agent for *HaMossad leMonddiin uleTafkidim Meyuhadim*. *Mossad*, the national Intelligence Agency of Israel, had been a good fit for him. In this capacity he had been instrumental in recruiting Ty and Regan to assist him in protecting the State of Israel from danger. Close calls and near-death disasters had formed a deep bond of friendship between the three in a short period of time.

After silently admiring the glowing dawn, Ty said, "Solly, would you excuse us? I'd like to show Regan the Northern Hanging Palace that Herod the Great built." Ty put his hand on the small of Regan's back and gently pressed.

Solly grinned and said, "Sure, mate. You kids run along. I'll be here when you get back."

As they walked on top of the massive rock formation that had served as Israel's fortress 2,000 years ago, Ty explained to Regan all about the excavations of the massive food storehouses and the ornate Roman baths King Herod had built on Masada when he used it as his private palatial retreat.

After walking for about a quarter-mile, they finally reached the northern cliff of Masada and walked down three series of wooden steps to reach the remains of Herod's magnificent residence. They stared out across the desert landscape, neither one speaking.

Ty turned to Regan and placed his hands on her shoulders.

"Regan..." he started.

As Ty held her at arm's length, Regan noticed moisture gathering in the corners of his blue eyes.

She smiled and said, "Yes, Ty?"

"I've known for a long time that I really care for you. But lately I've come to realize that I can't live without you. Will you marry me?" he said, cocking his head to one side.

"I will," she said coyly, "but on one condition."

"Name it."

"You drive on our honeymoon. I'm never flying with you again." The last time Regan had been in a plane with Ty had nearly ended their relationship in more than one way.

Ty grinned and said, "Deal!" Then he leaned in, embraced Regan, and tenderly lowered his lips toward hers.

"And here's a kiss to seal the deal," he said. Regan closed her eyes, ready to bask in the warmth of his embrace and the taste of their first kiss.

As their lips met, they jumped when they heard a

series of muffled "whumps!" They jerked their heads to the sky in time to see dozens of tiny explosive clouds leaving pockmarks on the sky. The strange phenomena appeared as tiny firework eruptions followed by blasts of white smoke. It was obvious that the detonations exploded at a very high altitude because the upper-level winds were already beginning to tear apart the circular shape of each blast.

"What was that?" Regan asked as a shiver tickled her spine.

Ty shielded his eyes and said, "I don't know. Some kind of explosion at a great altitude, I think." Knowing that sound travels slowly, Ty knew the blasts must have happened several seconds—maybe minutes—before they heard the noise.

With her arms still encircling Ty's neck, their mobile phones interrupted them with insistent buzzing.

Both frowned and said simultaneously, "Do you ever turn that thing off?"

They laughed together and fished out their phones in a friendly race to see who could check theirs first.

There was a message blinking on their screens that they had never seen before. It read:

No Service. The cellular grid is inoperable.

They tried swiping up on the screen to access the functions of their smartphone, but it was locked.

"What's up with this?" Ty asked. "I've never seen a message like that before. Have you?"

Regan shook her head. "Nope. That's the first time. Let's try rebooting our phones to see if we can fix it."

Ty tapped at the screen and said, "I can't get my phone to turn off, can you?"

"No. That's odd."

After a few moments of furtive attempts, Ty said, "That darn warning is still on the screen, and it's stuck. It's like someone has hacked into the entire system."

"You may be right. Let's go check with Solly."

They started running up the wooden staircase, noting the air was punctuated with the whine of turbine-driven helicopters. Three rotary-wing aircraft roared over their heads traveling south.

Ty looked up and said, "Those are Israeli military helicopters. Sikorsky UH-60s. Something is going on. Let's find Solly!"

They broke into a trot heading back to the entrance where they had left Solly. When they came in sight of the area, one of the helicopters quickly touched down amid a tornado of dust churned from its downwash. The other two helicopters hovered around the landing in protective formation. Through the cloud of dust they watched as two Israeli airmen climbed out and quickly took Solly on board. As soon as he was inside, all three helicopters roared toward the visitor parking area at the base of Masada. A commando jumped out of one of the helicopters, ran to Solly's Range Rover, and started the engine. The helicopters roared back into the sky, and soon Solly's SUV was throwing up a rooster tail of dust as it sped back toward the main road.

Within moments, the desert had absorbed the sound of the helicopters, and Ty and Regan stood side-by-side speechless.

Regan said, "There goes our guide and our ride. What are we going to do?"

"Let's head back down to the parking lot. I've got a bad feeling about this!"

As Regan followed behind Ty down the winding trail, she wondered, "Wait a second. Did he really just propose to me?"

3

Masada, Near the Judean Desert

A wry smile peeked out from Solly's thick beard as he watched Ty and Regan walking toward the ruins of Herod's hanging palace. *"It's about time the bloke popped the question to Regan,"* he thought to himself. *"I can't believe he's waited this long. A mate would have to be a shingle short of a roof not to see that they are made for each other."*

Solly settled down on one of the benches in the covered areas where tour guides always explained the layout of Masada to tourists. He was tempted to check his cell phone for messages or emails, but instead, he decided to close his eyes and relax for a few minutes. The last few weeks had been packed with action and tension. Most of the world's population were clueless about how close ISIS had come to destroying Jerusalem and much of the surrounding territories.

"I could sure use a vacation," he told himself. He laid

back and covered his face with his Stetson hat and crossed his boots, hoping to get a little shut-eye until the lovebirds returned.

Solly was uncertain how long he had been dozing when an alarm on his cell phone rudely interrupted his nap. He sat up and looked at the screen.

No Service. The cellular grid is inoperable.

"That's odd. Never seen that message before," he said aloud. Solly had never known the Israeli cellular system to fail before. Due to the fact that Israel's enemies were a constant threat, the civilian system had back-ups and redundant safeguards.

While he was staring at the screen, his phone started beeping rapidly. Solly understood that this was the Push to Talk System that all Israeli Secret Services employed for emergencies. Rather than using a cellular system, this PTT communication operated on a military grid. Each phone had been configured with a top-secret app that was activated in the case of an emergency.

"What's going on now?" Solly thought. When he stared up at the morning sky, his jaw dropped. He gazed at the dozens of circular cloud formations dotting the sky. *"What in blazes is that?"*

When the beeping from his phone stopped, there was a flashing icon on the screen. He pushed it and said, "Agent Ruben here. What's the status?"

Solly recognized the voices of Asher Hazzan, the Director of *Mossad*, and Natan Abrams, the Prime Minister.

"Solly, it's Asher and Natan here," Natan said.

"Go ahead, sir. What's going on?"

Natan asked Asher to continue. "We suspect that some terrorist group just detonated a series of EMPs somewhere in the atmosphere. The electromagnetic pulse has crippled all of our civilian communications. We're still assessing the damage, but it appears that they targeted our nation at our Global Positioning System."

Solly wasn't surprised because he had been briefed about this potential threat to Israel's GPS. "Who has the technology to do this to us?" The other option was that a group had developed the capability enough to have it stolen away from them by another group and executed.

Natan interrupted, "We'll talk about this when you arrive in Jerusalem. I've already dispatched three IDF helicopters. Before the GPS system went down, we tracked you to Masada. Just stay there. The ETA is in six minutes. We have a meeting scheduled as soon as you arrive."

Solly protested, "But what about my American friends? They are here with me."

"Sorry," Asher snapped. "They'll just have to fend for themselves. This is a national emergency."

They terminated the connection and Solly could already hear the distant sound of the Sikorsky UH-60s as their blades beat a furious pace through the air.

Solly walked out to a flatter area on top of Masada and said aloud, "And I thought today was going to be a holiday."

4

Masada, Near the Judean Desert

It took Ty and Regan only about thirty minutes to scramble down the Snake Path to the base of Masada. The massive visitor's center wouldn't open for another hour. A lone building in the desolate Judean desert, it rose out of the rock as an otherworldly apparition. The cable cars that would soon carry hundreds of tourists to the top of Masada hung motionless in mid-air.

Regan was tired and thirsty now. She bent over and placed both hands on the hem of her shorts to catch her breath. Glancing up at Ty, she pulled tendrils of her long blonde hair out of her face and asked, "Okay, Mr. Smart Guy. What's next?"

"We'd better get hydrated, or we won't last long in this place," Ty said, eyeing an outdoor faucet for tourist to fill their water bottles in the courtyard beside the locked doors to the museum, gift shops, and restaurants. They walked over, and both drank until they were full and washed their face and necks in the cool water.

"I wish we had something to carry water," Ty said, looking around.

Regan had already made her way over to one of the large plastic garbage receptacles. "Let's hope that they didn't remove the trash from yesterday." She opened the lid and turned her head away, "Ooh. That's pretty stinky. But here goes."

Regan held her nose and ferreted through the trash container before coming up with a used plastic water bottle in each hand. "Beggars can't be choosers. Let's rinse these out and fill them."

Ty took the bottles and started to rinse them under the faucet. "I never knew you were a dumpster diver," he chided her.

"I have skills that you can't even imagine," she quipped. And Ty knew that was true. Regan had surprised him on more than one occasion with the ingenuity and resourcefulness of a spy, although she was just a software developer.

They started the trek down the access road to the main highway that ran alongside the Dead Sea. It took them another ten minutes, and already half their water was gone.

"I figure when we get to the highway, we can hitch

a ride back to civilization," Ty said.

"Well, how many vehicles have you seen pass by in the last ten minutes?" Regan asked.

"Uh, I haven't been counting."

"Well, I have. And the total is zero. Something is going on. And I have a bad feeling about it."

"Well," Ty said, "I know we can't walk back to Jerusalem. It's too far. But if we head south, we can be at the Dead Sea spa hotels in about two or three hours."

"I think that's the better option," Regan agreed. "And I could sure use a spa treatment about now!"

As they turned south to walk along the highway, Ty looked across the road at the private airstrip that ran parallel to the highway. "That's the Bar Yehuda Airport named in honor of Israel bar Yehuda, one of the first Israeli freedom fighters. Here's a little trivia for you. What makes this airstrip unique among all the airports in the world?"

Regan smiled and said, "I would guess that it is the most deserted airport in the world."

"Nope," Ty said. "The thing that makes this airport unique is that it is 1,250 feet below sea level. It's the lowest elevation of any airport in the world. If you took off from here, you'd have to climb to over a thousand feet just to get to sea level."

Regan sped up her pace and said, "Thank you, Mr.

Trivial Pursuit. I'll remember that for future reference."
Ty was full of useless knowledge.

As they continued to walk down the road, Ty
spotted a tiny hangar near the end of the runway.

"Hey, wait a minute," he said. "Let's check out that
hangar. You never know. There might be a phone in
there, a car, or even a plane."

"No, thanks. I've had it with you and airplanes,"
Regan complained. "The last time I was in an airplane
with you, we crashed in a field in Texas."

Ty corrected her. "We didn't crash. We made an
emergency landing in a farmer's field. Any landing
you walk away from is a good one."

"I promised the Lord that if I could survive that
crash, then I'd never fly in another airplane where you
were the pilot."

"Come on," Ty argued, grabbing her elbow and
pulling her off the road. "Let's check it out at least."

After picking their way carefully through a maze
of scrub plants and sharp rocks, they arrived at the
runway. The single metal hangar wasn't new, but it
didn't look deserted either. A faded sign read, "Masada
Sightseeing Tours."

Ty saw that the two sliding doors were connected
by a thick chain secured by a large, black padlock. He
forced the two doors apart by a few inches and peered
inside. "It's hard to see, but I think there's something

in there."

Regan said, "Well, great. But unless you are Houdini and can pick that lock, we don't have any way to get in."

"Don't forget. I was an airport rat. I grew up around airports and hangars in East Texas. Most plane owners I know usually hide a spare key somewhere. Let's look around."

They began to look for obvious places for a key. Ty turned over several large rocks and walked all the way around the building without uncovering a spare key. When he arrived back at the front, Regan was standing there leaning against the hangar door.

Ty shook his head. "I guess this is a dry well. No key. So I guess we go back to walking south."

Regan held up a key and said, "I started to throw this little guy into the desert, but I decided to see what you can do with it."

"Where did you find it?" Ty asked, taking the key out of her hand.

"The first place I looked," Regan replied smartly. "It was hanging on the backside of the sightseeing tours sign."

"You are not only beautiful. You are a genius, too!"

"Keep it up," Regan said as she fitted the key into the rusty padlock and jiggled it until the lock snapped open. "Flattery will get you everywhere."

5

The Knesset, Jerusalem

On the quick flight from the desert, Solly learned more intel that *Mossad* had gathered about the EMP attack. The Electromagnetic Pulse bombs had exploded in the upper atmosphere, damaging almost all electronic communications in Israel. The spillover from the attack was also affecting Lebanon, Syria, Jordan, and parts of Egypt. Solly knew that Lebanon and Syria lacked the technology to carry out such an attack. And he quickly deduced that the other affected countries couldn't be responsible because they would not have crippled their own communications systems.

He then began mentally eliminating the six nations that had formed a historic peace alliance with Israel months earlier. The Middle Eastern Peace Alliance (MEPA) was comprised of Jordan, Israel, Egypt, Turkey, The Saudi Kingdom, The United Arab Emirates, and Qatar. Their partnership had brokered an unexpected peace treaty between Israel and the Arab nations aligned against the scourge of ISIS.

Solly looked out the window and saw downtown Jerusalem. Two of the Sikorsky helicopters hovered around the Knesset, Israel's parliament in Western Jerusalem. The third helicopter carrying Solly swooped into the landing area. Solly was quickly disgorged like an unwanted trespasser.

Before his boots hit the pavement, two IDF soldiers were on either side, running him toward the private VIP entrance and into the Prime Minister's office. Natan Abrams was seated around a conference table with Asher Hazzan to his right. The other members seated around the table were a who's who of Israeli military and intelligence services. Natan got right to the point.

"Solly, be seated. We're on a conference call with President Turner in Washington." Natan turned back to the video conference screen and said, "President Turner, please continue your briefing."

President David Turner wasn't a typical Washington politician. He had a military and academic background as a retired career Army Colonel who had taught at West Point Military Academy. He had also been tapped to serve as the president of Texas A&M University in College Station. As a young man serving in local Texas politics, he had been appointed by Texas Governor Hugh Packard to complete the unexpired term of Senator Wayne Compton who had dropped dead on the Senate floor with a brain aneurysm.

Senator Turner brought a no-nonsense approach to government that ignored the typically heated party animosity. He was known to cross the aisle to vote on issues that he considered the right thing to do and eventually gained the respect and grudging admiration of both parties. When running for President of the United States, many considered him a long shot for the party's primary, but he was nominated on the first ballot. He squeaked out an electoral college win that caused many of his opponents to call for a recount that was later denied. While his opponents complained incessantly and even brought lawsuits against him, President Turner got down to the business of running the country.

One of his first acts as president was to give the military the full authority to make decisions regarding the fight against ISIS. Within eighteen months of being elected, ISIS had been reduced to a few remote cells. He was a friend of Israel and had long recognized Jerusalem as the capital of Israel. In his first year of office, he moved the United States Embassy there as a show of support.

He was the right man at the right time to deal with

this new terrorist act. As President Turner looked into the camera, he said, "We have confirmation from the CIA that the origin of the rockets carrying the EMP bombs originated in southern Iran. There were fifteen different heat signatures from launches that occurred almost simultaneously. Dr. Thomas Wagner, a NASA scientist, can give you more information on exactly how they were able to dismantle communication systems in Israel so quickly."

The camera panned left to Dr. Wagner, a thirty-something man who looked as if he should be playing in the NFL rather than working with NASA. Wagner had starred as a linebacker for the MIT Engineers. But he felt more at home with quantum physics than blitz packages.

Dr. Wagner began, "I feel I should start with some important context for what we've discovered. As most of you know, the U.S. Air Force first started researching satellite-based navigation in the 1960s. The Global Positioning System was first launched in 1974 when NASA launched the first of 24 proposed satellites that would be stationed in space in a geosynchronous earth orbit—or GEO for short. In other words, they would rotate at the same speed as the daily rotation of the earth. Currently, the U.S. Air Force manages a constellation of 31 operational satellites. For the first twenty years, GPS was only used for U.S. military purposes. However, shortly after the Russians shot down Korean Air flight 007 in 1983 when it wandered off course into Soviet airspace, President Reagan offered to let all commercial aircraft utilize the GPS system. Does everyone follow me so far?"

President Turner said, "Yes, and thanks for the background. Let's get to the point of today's attack."

Dr. Wagner continued calmly, "Yes, Mr. President. Since GPS became available to civilians, it has become the standard for everything from aviation to GPS location using cell phones. However, some countries, including Russia, China, Japan, and India have launched similar satellite systems that they only employ for military use. Israel, for example, has developed IRENA—Israel Regional Navigation Satellite System. It consists of single mother satellite and four smaller daughter satellites in GEO. This system is in a lower orbit than the original GPS satellites which orbit the earth at an altitude of about 12,000 miles, which we consider to be Medium Earth Orbit. The Israeli system is in Low Earth Orbit. This is why the electronics were fried by the EMP bombs. The added damage to the electrical grid and cellular system was a by-product of this event."

President Turner interrupted. "Mr. Prime Minister, our military and C.I.A. are convinced that Iran is behind this attack."

Solly drew a deep breath. If this was true, things could get ugly quickly in the Middle East.

Natan said, "Ordinarily, this outrageous attack would only be a major inconvenience, like a computer hack. However, when the EMP bomb exploded, our military aircraft temporarily lost their navigational instruments. Two of our F-15E Strike fighter jets were on training maneuvers in a tight formation in the clouds. When they lost all navigation, there was a collision and all four pilots ejected. The aircraft were lost and two of our pilots didn't survive. They were struck by shrapnel from the exploding fighter jets. I blame Iran on this unprovoked attack and we will answer back with force."

President Turner continued, "Mr. Prime Minister, please accept my condolences for the loss of your pilots. This is an outrageous act. We have launched a protest to their government through the Swiss Embassy. We haven't heard a response from them yet. However, we want to confirm that we consider an attack against Israel to be an attack against the United States. In the meantime, we have changed the transponder codes for the military use of our GPS system and are making it available to the Israeli government so you won't be flying blind."

Prime Minister Abrams said, "Thank you for the briefing, Mr. President. We will be in consultation with you and your intelligence services about a response."

"Thank you, Mr. Prime Minister," President Turner said. "You and your citizens are in our prayers."

"Shalom," said Natan.

He nodded at the technician who killed the live video feed. Then he turned to the group and said, "As you well know, Israel will not stand by when we are attacked. We will rise up and kill our enemies before they cross our borders. Asher, I want an operative plan on my desk first thing in the morning."

Asher returned to his office down the hall and shut the door. He put his phone on "do not disturb" and closed his eyes. It was time for some bold and unexpected action. Something like the raid on Entebbe. His mind wandered back to his unforgettable first mission as a young Israeli commando in 1976.

6

Tel Aviv

It began as a routine Air France flight from Tel Aviv to Paris. Air France flight 139 was an Airbus 300 that lifted off from Ben Gurion airport on time carrying 247 passengers and thirteen crew members. The flight proceeded for a scheduled stop at Athens, Greece, before continuing on to Paris. While the aircraft was in the Greek capital, four passengers boarded who were members of the Popular Front for the Liberation of Palestine. The world would later learn that two of the hijackers were Palestinian and two were German. Due to non-existent airport security, they were carrying weapons and explosives in their carryon bags.

Four minutes after lifting off from Athens, the pilots heard shouting from the cabin. The captain sent the flight engineer to investigate. When the flight engineer opened the cockpit door, he was met by one of the German hijackers holding a grenade. He pointed a gun at the engineer's head and forced his way into the cockpit. Then he took aim at the captain's head.

In seconds, the hijacker had pulled the first officer out of his seat, throwing him toward the back of the cockpit. He ordered the first officer and the flight engineer into the passenger section, closed the cockpit door, and settled into the co-pilot's seat with a gun still pointed at the Air France captain.

In a thick German accent, he announced that the flight would now be called Haifa 1, taking the name of the seacoast city the Palestinians claimed as their own. His demands included the release of 53 Palestinian prisoners held in in five different countries. The hijacker also commanded the captain to reroute the aircraft to Benghazi, Libya.

The hijacker took the microphone and read a lengthy tribute to Muammar Gaddafi before the flight landed in Benghazi. Once it refueled, the aircraft took off again. The captain tentatively asked the hijacker where they were heading now and received a chilling reply.

"It's not your business," the terrorist seethed.

Eventually, the pilot was instructed to fly to Entebbe airport in Uganda, Africa. When the plane landed and taxied to the terminal, the terrified passengers were greeted by a chilling sight. The notorious dictator, Idi Amin, was standing on the tarmac dressed in his trademark camouflage battle fatigues. All passengers, who now realized they were hostages, were escorted off the plane and into the old terminal building.

The hijackers and Ugandan soldiers separated the Israeli citizens and several non-Israeli Jews from the rest of the passengers. Eventually, 148 non-Jewish passengers were released and flown to Paris. Ninety-four Jewish hostages, along with the Air France crew who refused to leave the passengers, remained.

Back in Israel, military planners were unwilling to concede the demands of the hijackers and adhered to a strict policy of not negotiating with terrorists. Eitan Barr served as the strategist during the crisis, overseeing all the planning for the complex rescue operation. As other soldiers gathered in a strategy session in Tel Aviv, most of those present had no clue where Entebbe was even located.

As they began to plan the operation, an Israeli engineer came forward. He had designed floor plans for the new terminal at Entebbe. Providentially, he also had stashed in his files the floor plans for the old terminal where the hostages were being held.

Barr told his team. "We won't just be dealing with

the four hijackers. The madman, Idi Amin, and his forces have joined forces with the hijackers. Prepare to interface with the entire Ugandan military."

Among the plans discussed was the idea of parachuting Israeli Navy SEALS into Lake Victoria near the airport. They also considered landing in Kenya and utilizing a speedboat to reach Entebbe. Various additional plans were offered and eliminated. If they didn't come up with a viable rescue plan soon, they would be forced to negotiate with the terrorists.

Meanwhile, inside the old terminal in Entebbe, the hijackers yelled constantly at the Jewish hostages and threatened to shoot them. For many of the hostages, this brought back horrible memories of the way Jews were rounded up and killed by the Nazis.

One of the passengers later recounted, "It was like the death camps. The Germans decided who would live and who would die. It was very frightening."

The Air France pilot, Michel Bacos, would later recall, "Time slowed to a crawl. The adults tried to distract the children with bottle tops and cigarette cartons turned into toys; they'd also work shifts, cleaning up or stretching out the food to make it last, and assembling a library of the books they had imagined reading on the flight. They slept an hour or two, lights on all night. There were a lot of mosquitoes and flies. The smell was terrible. No clothes to change into. No water."

A hostage who was only thirteen at the time would later write, "Our greatest horror were the daily visits of Amin and his entourage when the dictator would address the hostages. He would deliver long monologues, never allowing the hostages to speak. His sheer size was terrifying to the children. We would cower near the wall, looking at Amin's son, wife, and aides. They're all in the shade when you're standing close to Idi Amin: he's simply gigantic."

Back in Tel Aviv, a plan was being finalized. The latest intel had discovered that Idi Amin was leaving the country the next weekend for a diplomatic trip. Barr explained a daring plan to fly four huge Hercules transports 2,500 miles to Uganda. One of the aircraft would unload a motorcade of soldiers disguised to appear as the dictator and his military entourage returning from their trip. The ruse would distract and confuse the guards. This would buy some time at the airport for the other aircraft to land and deploy the rest of the Israeli soldiers who raid the terminal where the hostages were being held. The planning required the acquisition of a rare Mercedes limousine like Amin's. The Israelis eventually located one, but it was the wrong color. They hastily painted it black, like the extravagant dictator's, and prepared to put the implausible plan into action.

7

JULY 4, 1976
Uganda

On Saturday night, July 4, 1976, while Americans were celebrating 200 years of independence, the Israelis were launching the most daring rescue operation in modern history. Eitan Barr appointed Yoni Abrams, a military strategist and the older brother of future Israeli Prime Minister Natan Abrams, to lead the mission. Asher Hazzan was among the first young commandos who would land and pose as Ugandan forces.

The four Hercules military transports would be joined by two Boeing 707 jets. One would serve as a flying command post, and one would serve as a field hospital. The Israeli medical personnel were prepared to treat the wounded and retrieve the dead from the risky rescue. Two hundred Israeli soldiers would support the rescue mission.

As the four massive aircraft approached Africa after an eight-hour flight, they descended to treetop level to avoid radar detection. The turbulence at that low altitude was severe, causing nausea and vomiting onboard.

Soon Entebbe came into view. As planned, the aircraft would land in total darkness on the unlit single runway. The first Hercules touched down, and the reverse thrusters brought the mammoth plane to a sudden stop. The cargo door dropped, and a black limousine sped out of the plane, followed by other vehicles in a motorcade. The Israelis desperately hoped to maintain the precious advantage of surprise, but a single Ugandan soldier appeared and raised his weapon. The Israelis fired their silenced pistols, and the armed man fell. When he climbed back to his feet, an Israeli soldier fired a loud shot from a rifle, losing the element of surprise for the entire mission.

Over the next thirty minutes, the Israelis and Ugandan forces engaged in a vicious firefight. The occupants of the Mercedes continued toward the terminal and jumped out to enter the area occupied by the hijackers and hostages.

As the rescue team burst into the terminal, the hijackers had little time to shoot any of the hostages. Instead, Israeli commandos began firing at the men holding weapons. One by one, the hijackers collapsed on the floor, along with several Ugandan soldiers. Meanwhile an Israeli soldier carrying a battery-powered megaphone shouted to the hostages in English and Hebrew, "Lie down! Don't get up! The army is here! The army is here!"

All the hostages complied instantly and fell prostrate, covering their heads with their hands and pulling children underneath them. Then it was suddenly quiet. When the Israeli soldier with the megaphone saw that all the hijackers had been killed, he said in a calm voice, "We've come to take all of you home."

In the fierce fighting, all the hijackers were killed, along with twenty Ugandan soldiers. Of the 106 hostages, three were killed. One person was left in Uganda for medical reasons, and ten passengers were injured. Commander Yoni Abrams had also been shot in the rescue attempt.

The Israeli soldiers gently escorted the remaining hostages onboard the Hercules transports. The four aircraft loaded with Israeli soldiers and grateful passengers climbed to a safe altitude and flew to Nairobi, Kenya, where those in need of medical attention were treated for injuries and trauma.

Commander Yoni was treated by a combat medic throughout the flight to Nairobi. About thirty minutes after they touched down, the Jewish hero died in the arms of the medic.

Asher Hazzan made an interesting observation in the official debrief document he composed after the raid. He wrote, "I was struck by the contrasting mood on board. The hostages were celebrating just one hour after their liberation. Their mood was one of ecstatic joy and relief. But my fellow commanders were far from happy. We were exhausted and saddened by the death of our commander, Yoni."

Asher had never forgotten the lessons learned from that fateful mission. And now he was facing a situation that called for the same sort of creative courage Israel had exhibited that night.

8

Bar Jehuda Airport
Masada, Israel

Ty removed the chain that was holding the two hangar doors together. He placed his left shoulder against one of the doors and pushed. The door didn't budge.

"Can you give me a little help here?" Ty grunted as he strained against the door. "I think the rail and wheels on this door may be a little rusty."

"Sure," Regan purred. "Bring in the muscle for a man's job."

Regan pushed lower on the door, and Ty labored above her to budge the obstinate door. Gradually, they felt the door start to move. The metal wheels on the rails screeched like giant fingernails scratching a blackboard.

"There! We've got it. Keep pushing!" Ty groaned.

As the door gained momentum, they were able to move it all the way to the end of the hangar. As they stopped to catch their breath, Regan glanced at the interior. Sitting there like a lost pet canary was a tiny yellow airplane.

She pointed at the plane and laughed. "Is that a model airplane? Or is it for real? Either way, you're not getting me in that teeny death trap!"

A huge smile broke out on Ty's face. "That, my lady, is a classic. It is a venerable Piper Cub."

"Well, I agree it's a cub. But I will only fly in the full-grown version, thank you." Regan crossed her arms and pretended to pout.

"Regan, it's one of the most popular airplanes ever made! It was produced in the 1930s and 40s. Many pilots grew up getting their first flights in a Cub. There were a couple of Cubs at Pounds Field in Tyler where I grew up, so I have a few hours in them. Here, let's roll back the other door so we can get this little guy outside."

The second door wasn't as hard to move, so they slowly pushed it until it reached the end of the track.

Regan walked over to examine the small plane. It was sitting on two large tires with a small tailwheel at the back. She said, "It looks like it's only big enough for one passenger. That's fine with me. You go fly and get us some help. I'll wait right here."

Ty said, "Nope. It's a two-passenger airplane. The pilot and passenger sit in tandem. Your first class seat is the one in back."

Regan ran her hand over the fuselage of the aircraft. "Wait a minute! This plane isn't even made of metal. This feels like cloth! You expect me to fly in a plane that is covered with the same fabric that I'm wearing?"

"Settle down," he said. "The Cub has a sturdy steel frame covered with thick canvas that has been treated with a poly-urethane paint called 'dope.' That thickens and strengthens the fabric while giving it the advantage of being much lighter than metal surfaces."

"I caught that, mister. You must think I'm the dope for refusing to fly in a plane covered with treated bedsheets!" Regan said, turning up the corner of her mouth to betray the fact that she was kidding.

Ty didn't catch this nuance, however, so he launched into his defense as usual. "Regan, be reasonable! There have been thousands of these planes flying for decades. And there have only been a few crashes. Almost everyone survives a crash in a Cub because it's never going fast enough to really create a danger!"

Regan gave in. "Okay, flyboy. I'm convinced. So how do we fly this Dreamliner?"

Ty smiled, feeling relieved. "Well, we may not fly it. We don't know how long it's been since it flew. I have to check it out and ensure everything is working, including having enough fuel and oil."

"What are you waiting for?" Regan asked.

Ty walked over to the hangar wall and hit the light switch. Nothing happened. "Whatever messed up our cellphones looks like it's affecting the electricity too. Let's pull the Cub out into the light."

Ty reached up and grabbed the propeller near the central spinner and started walking backward. He easily pulled the Cub out of the hangar by himself.

"That plane must be very light!" Regan observed.

"It doesn't weigh much at all. If I recall, it weighs around 700 pounds when it is full of fuel."

Ty continued to pull the little tailwheel aircraft out until it was near the runway. He walked beside it and yelled to Regan, "Hey, I saw a stepladder stacked in the corner of the hangar. Will you bring it to me?"

Regan found the aluminum stepladder in the dark corner and brought it out to the plane. Ty positioned the ladder in front of the cockpit behind the propeller.

"I thought airplanes carried their fuel in the wings," Regan noted.

"Most of them do," Ty explained. "But the old Piper Cub has one gas tank right here between the cockpit and the engine."

He climbed up the ladder and removed the gas cap. He withdrew the cap with a long metal rod attached with a cork at the end. "It's kind of old-fashioned, but that's the gas gauge. If the cork is wet, there's fuel."

He smelled the cork. "The good news is, there's some fuel in the tank. But I don't know how much there is."

Ty began to rock the light aircraft. "I'm giving it the 'slosh test.' If I can hear some fuel sloshing around, I can get an idea of how much fuel we have. The Cub holds about twelve gallons. It sounds like it's less than half-full."

"How far can that get us, assuming you can get this thing started and in the air?" Regan asked.

"Well, I think it burns about four gallons an hour, so I'd say we have around an hour's flying time. She doesn't go fast—her top speed is about 80 mph. I can remember flying a Cub in East Texas and looking down to see cars going faster than I was!"

Regan laughed.

"But that should be enough fuel to get us near civilization," he added. "Let me check the oil level." He removed the oil stick and saw that there was plenty of oil for four cylinders to have enough lubrication to produce the expected 85 horsepower. "I think we're good to go. Hop in the back seat."

9

Bar Jehuda Airport
Masada, Israel

Regan stared at the tiny light aircraft and crossed her arms in defiance. "You really think I'm going to get in that toy airplane?"

Ty shot her his most confident smile.

"Can you just trust me for once?"

"I've heard you say those words too many times. It's a miracle I'm still alive after trusting some of your crazy ideas."

Ty's smile tightened.

"That's exactly what I'm saying," he countered. "You are still alive. I haven't killed you yet..." *Although there have been some tough calls*, he wanted to add.

"Listen," he continued, "if we don't get in this plane and get back to where we can contact people we're going to face a long, hot day. Something big is going on and we've got to find Solly to get the latest intel."

Regan held up her index finger. "Okay. Just once more. I'll trust you."

She gingerly climbed into the tiny rear cockpit and noticed the only controls included a stick protruding between her legs, two pedals under her feet, and two short levers on the left side.

Ty made his way up the ladder, leaned over the front cockpit, and turned a switch. He adjusted a couple of the levers on the left side of the cockpit. Then he climbed back down and removed the stepladder.

"Are you ready to go?" he asked, standing beside her.

"You tell me. I'm not flying this thing. When are you going to climb in and start it? Regan said.

"This thing doesn't have an electric starter. And it's probably a good thing since everything electric seems to be on the fritz. You crank this baby with some muscle power. Have you ever seen a prop start?"

"I'm not liking the sound of this," Regan protested. "Do you mean you're going to be on the outside when the plane starts? What if it starts moving and I'm the only one in it?"

"Your part is very important, Regan. I've turned on the magnetos and enriched the fuel. I've opened the throttle just a little. That's the larger lever to your right. Put your feet on the two pedals on the floor.

Those are the rudder pedals—and the brakes. I need you to press your feet on the top of the pedals so the plane won't move after I've started the engine. Got it?"

Regan looked nervous. "Ty, I don't know. I've never done this before. I've heard of people being killed by a propeller. Be careful."

"Don't worry. I know what I'm doing," Ty told her. He'd never actually hand-propped a Cub, but he'd seen it done a few times.

Ty walked around the front and placed the palms of his hands on one side of the two-bladed propeller.

"Brake on!" he shouted.

"Brake on!" Regan repeated, pushing the pedals down.

Ty lifted his left leg to get momentum and spun the propeller downward. It caught for a second and then reversed direction for a full turn. "Don't worry. You usually have to do it several times," he yelled.

"Brake on!" he said again.

"Brake on!" Regan responded. Already her legs were beginning to be sore from the extreme pressure she was putting on the brakes.

Ty spun the propeller again. This time it circled twice and then stopped immediately. He repeated these steps a third time before the engine emitted a thin cough, and the propeller stopped.

"Okay!" he yelled. "We have fuel in the cylinders

now. This time, as soon as I spin the propeller, advance the large lever to your left. Don't push it all the way. Just move it forward a couple of inches."

He spun the propeller with the greatest exertion yet. It paused for a moment before the engine roared into life. The propeller was spinning, but something was wrong. The plane was moving toward him at a rapid pace. Ty jumped to the side just in time to avoid the deadly propeller. Then he rolled to avoid being run over by the left wheel. He looked up and saw the plane was taxiing ahead full speed!

He jumped to his feet and ran beside the plane until he caught up with it. Regan had a look of sheer terror on her face. She turned to look at him as if to say, "What do I do now?"

Over the roar of the engine, Ty yelled, "Pull back on the lever! Then step on the brakes—hard!"

Regan had the presence of mind to pull back gently on the throttle, and the engine settled down. Then she stomped on the brakes so hard that the plane stopped and the tail rose off the ground. She was afraid that the little plane would flip right over, but after suspending in the air, the tail settled back to the pavement with a thud.

"Great job, Regan!" Ty said, climbing into the front cockpit to take over.

Regan said nothing. She was just trying to breathe.

With sweat streaming down his face, he reacquainted himself with the four basic instruments on the panel. The plane didn't have a radio, but the previous pilot had mounted a small Garmin handheld GPS on the dash. Fortunately, it was powered by the alternator that was driven by the engine.

Ty shouted over his shoulder, "We're good to go. We even have a GPS receiver. It will take us straight to our destination."

"What is our destination?" Regan yelled back.

"Uh. I'm not sure. Let me look on the GPS. It should list all the nearest airports." Ty watched as the GPS powered up. The screen read: "Acquiring satellites." He waited for a few more minutes until the message appeared: "No satellites available."

"That's strange," Ty thought. He'd been flying for twenty years and had never had a GPS fail to find satellites. Something odd was going on.

"Well, we aren't going to sit here burning precious fuel," he told himself. *"I can find a town using good ol' IFR navigation."*

In aviation terminology, that meant "Instrument Flight Rules." But when you're flying a stripped-down Cub, pilots like to joke that it stands for "I Follow Roads."

Ty calculated that the prevailing wind was from the south, so he pressed the left rudder pedal to turn left and taxi to the end of the runway. Once there, he punched the right rudder and turned the airplane until it was facing south.

He slowly advanced the throttle. "Here we go!" he shouted.

The Piper Cub Ty flew was typically a short takeoff and landing aircraft in normal conditions. But at the lowest spot on the planet, the thicker atmosphere increased the lift performance of the airplane's fat wings. After traveling only about fifteen seconds down the runway, the canary-colored Cub sprang into the air and found its wings.

Ty turned left until he was heading north. He wanted to gain plenty of altitude over the Dead Sea before turning west to cross the rising terrain of the Judean mountains. For the first time that day, he let out a quiet sigh of relief. Just then he felt an assuring hand reach over from the rear cockpit squeeze his shoulder.

10

The sky above the Dead Sea

As Ty flew north, he continued to gain altitude, keeping a gentle backward pressure on the control stick. His eyes darted from the windscreen to the vertical speed indicator which was pegged at a steady climb of 500 feet per minute. After a couple of minutes, he turned the Piper Cub left until the magnetic compass read 270 degrees. As he leveled the wings he glanced left to look at the massive plateau of Masada. He knew that the top of Masada where they'd just been hours ago was roughly at sea level. When he reached an altitude close to Herod's majestic hanging palace, he twisted the altimeter to read zero. Masada viewed from the air was a rare sight.

Ty couldn't communicate with Regan in the rear seat because of the roar of the little engine. So, he turned around and pointed to the left so that she could take in the view. He soon reached an altitude of 4,500 feet above sea level. When he leveled off he was already well above the Judean mountains, and he could already see the shining city of Jerusalem less than twenty miles ahead.

He knew he could make it to Jerusalem, but he didn't know where to go once he arrived. He glanced down between his legs to see if there was a sectional chart or map. While his head was down, he suddenly felt Regan's hand slapping his right shoulder. He could barely make out her voice as she yelled, "We've got company!"

Ty looked to his right and was shocked to see an AH-64 Apache attack helicopter flying level with him. The weapons officer had the M230 chain gun aimed at Ty's tiny airplane. From his days as a Marine Corp pilot, Ty knew that the remotely controlled gun could fire 30mm bullets at over 600 rounds a minute. His pulse rate rammed up and perspiration broke out on his face.

Behind him, he heard Regan yelling above the drone of the engine, "They have a big gun pointing at us, so you'd better do something fast!"

He had no way to communicate with the Israeli flyer, so he quickly wagged his wings, the international sign acknowledging visual contact. The helicopter was so close he could see the pilot and the weapons officer looking at him.

Ty was out of options, so he quickly held up both hands making the sign of surrender.

The pilot nodded and circled his hand in a gesture to say, "Follow me."

Ty quickly saluted the helicopter pilot as the Apache attack helicopter pulled in front of the little Piper and began descending toward Jerusalem. The helicopter leveled off at 2,000 feet, so Ty also stopped his descent.

Just then he heard Regan shout, "There are two more with us now!"

Two additional attack helicopters had moved up on both sides of them. The helicopters were loaded with hellfire missiles underneath the fuselage. *"At least the guns aren't pointed at us,"* Ty thought with a sigh of relief.

The four aircraft continued their slow air parade north over a modern section of Jerusalem. Ty was amazed by the number of building cranes rising above the high-rise apartments under construction.

Just as he thought they were leaving Jerusalem air space, he glanced ahead and saw a runway on what appeared to be a deserted airport. Part of the single strip of concrete had caved in. Nevertheless, the lead Apache began descending toward the usable part of the runway and Ty followed. He saw members of the Israeli Defense Forces occupied some of the barracks around the crumbling terminal building.

Just before it reached the runway, the lead helicopter turned left and hovered in position. Ty gently descended until the Piper's two main landing gear tires made contact. He pulled back on the throttle and kept pressure on the rudder pedals until the tailwheel touched down. Before he could even think about where to taxi, two armed personnel carriers raced out to his position. The huge armored vehicles boasted eight tires and screeched to a halt beside the tiny aircraft. IDF soldiers immediately piled out with their weapons trained on the aircraft.

Ty pulled out the fuel mixture and the engine coughed once and then became silent. Ty said under his breath, "Ladies and gentlemen, welcome to Jerusalem. It's been our pleasure to be your airline of choice."

From behind him Regan whispered loudly, "That's not funny, buddy. And I'm *seriously* never going to fly with you again!"

As Ty raised the aircraft door to climb out, he looked up to see the familiar figure of Solly in his Stetson cowboy hat walking toward them across the broken pavement, a big smile emerging from his thick beard.

"I should have known you two would find a way back from the desert!" Solly called out to them.

Regan made her way out of the plane and said, "No thanks to you. What do you mean leaving us like that? We could have died." She looked around. "Where are we, and what in blazes is going on?"

"You've landed at what used to be the main airport for Jerusalem. It's called Atarot Airport. It's been shut down since 2001, but now it's occupied by our friendly members of the Israeli Defense Forces." He pointed to a tall fence surrounding the airfield. "Actually, everything on this side of that perimeter fence is in the West Bank, and our government decided to keep troops here to prevent the Palestinians from ever using it. It sure came in handy today for you two to find a safe landing."

Ty nodded eagerly, but Regan just grunted, nonplussed.

Solly motioned toward a black Land Rover that was idling behind the military vehicles. "Come with me, and I'll explain as much as I know about what's happening."

Solly climbed in behind the steering wheel, and Regan sat in the passenger seat. Ty scooted into the center of the backseat and said, "So what's going on?"

Solly drove around the military barracks and arrived at the security gate where a guard examined his credentials and looked suspiciously at the passengers. "They're with me. I'll vouch for them," Solly said with a smile.

He was waved through and started negotiating the sharp curves of the narrow roads in the northern edge of Jerusalem. "This is the latest," he began and explained that while they were on Masada this morning, the Iranians had exploded several Electromagnetic Pulse Bombs in the lower atmosphere. "Their target was to take down our satellite based navigation and communications system," Solly added. "I'm afraid we were caught off guard, and they not only knocked out our satellites but also fried our national cellular network."

"So that's why our phones don't work," Ty said.

Solly nodded. "That's true, but fortunately our military and intelligence services have an emergency communications system. It's a high-tech walkie-talkie system hardwired into all our phones and radios."

"When will our phones be working again?" Reagan asked.

"Our best tech guys are working hard on that and we believe it will be up and running by sunset today. We're not so fortunate on our satellites. But the Americans have given us access to their GPS satellites."

"So what kind of response is Israel planning?" Ty asked.

Solly shook his head. "I don't know yet. But it will

be more of a hammer instead of a feather. In addition to taking the satellites offline, the EMPS led to the collision of two of our F-15s. Two pilots died passing through the debris field when they ejected."

Ty let out a low whistle. "I wouldn't want to be any of the Iranian leaders right about now."

"The three of us are have a meeting with Director Hazzan tomorrow morning to discuss our options. I booked us rooms at the Waldorf Astoria Jerusalem. You both look like you could use a hot meal and a soft bed."

Ty chuckled, "That would be better than a hot bed and a soft meal!"

Regan was focused on her phone, but turned instinctively to swat Ty's leg. "Stop it!" she chided him. Suddenly she shouted, "Hey! Finally, some good news! My phone is working again!"

11

Bushehr Nuclear Power Plant
Bushehr, Iran

Nuclear physicist Dr. Parsa Turan inserted his keycard into the security slot under the watchful eye of a Revolutionary Guard soldier as he waited for the elevator to arrive. Parsa nodded at the soldier, but there was no response. He was the director of the Iranian Nuclear Agency, but he was awarded no special respect from the soldiers charged with guarding this strategic facility.

Parsa wore the keycard on a lanyard around his neck that also held his official identity badge. As the elevator door opened, Parsa glanced down at his tablet as if he were looking at important data. He was merely gazing at nothing to avoid the scrutiny of the guard. An imaginary worm of worry constantly bore a hole in his brilliant mind because of a secret he held. He knew that he would lose his life and his family would disappear if his superiors discovered his secret. He actually was guarding two secrets, but only one of them would get him killed.

Parsa worked at a facility that German contractors began building in 1975. Construction at the Bushehr Nuclear Power Plant in Southwestern Iran on the coast of the Persian Gulf was halted by the Islamic Revolution in Iran in 1979. During the revolution, the last monarch of Iran, Mohammed Reza Shah Pahlavi, was overthrown and exiled, and the Grand Ayatollah Ruholiah Khomeini was welcomed back to Iran by millions of Iranians. After a brief defense by a few troops loyal to the Shah, Khomeini established a new Islamic government and declared himself Supreme Leader in December of 1979.

Khomeini began to expel all foreigners and foreign companies. That fall young Islamists showing their allegiance to the Ayatollah invaded the U.S Government compound in Tehran and held fifty-two American diplomats as hostages for 444 days.

Meanwhile, the incomplete Bushehr Nuclear Power Plant would sit untouched like an ancient monolith in the desert for almost twenty years. Then in 1995, Iran signed an agreement with Russia and their nuclear power services contractor Atomstroyexport was hired to complete the site amid continual political and economic delays. Only by 2007 was the first nuclear material produced. The nuclear power plant began adding electricity to the national grid in 2011.

In 2014 Iran and Russian signed another agreement to build two more nuclear reactors at Bushehr. The agreement that was released named only two new reactors. But Russian President Michael Sokolov had conducted private negotiations with the Iranian government to build three additional underground halls to be utilized as uranium enrichment centers. These were constructed to enrich the uranium to weapons-grade level away from the eyes of the watching world. Weapons-grade uranium is highly enriched to over 90% U-235. Only at this level of enrichment does it become a fissile isotope required for a nuclear explosion.

The elevator descended a distance equal to a twenty-story building. The double doors silently slid open and Parsa passed through another security checkpoint. The armed guard standing there was not part of the Revolutionary Guard. He was a hardened member of VAJA, the Iranian Ministry of Intelligence. Only personnel with top secret clearance could access this area.

Parsa placed his hand on the fingerprint reader and the indicator turned green. The VAJA agent waved him through without a word. The secret enrichment area was housed under a massive underground bunker. While the other reactors above ground were producing electricity, these enrichment plants were hidden because they were illegal according to international sanctions.

In the last round of sanctions, the International Atomic Energy Agency had limited the amount of enriched uranium that Iran could obtain to only 300 kg. As head of this division Parsa, knew that Russia had secretly supplied an additional 1200 kg of uranium to be enriched. The vision of the current Great Leader, the Grand Ayatollah Savyid Ali Mazdaki, was to produce enough weapons-grade nuclear material to obliterate the nation of Israel. The Iranians were only weeks away from reaching that capability.

That was the secret that Parsa shared with the Great Leader and a few other Iranians who held top secret security clearance. However, it was his other secret that was bothering him most. As he walked toward his office he was tormented once again by his conflicting thoughts. He had always dreamed of becoming the top nuclear scientist in Iran. But on his way to this position, he made a career ending discovery: he had a conscience. He simply could not bear the idea of creating weapons to kill millions of innocent people.

He unlocked his office, turned on the lights,

and sat behind his desk. The pressures of his internal war with himself and the looming deadlines of his superiors to finish his work were building to a critical level. He crossed his arms on his desk and placed his head down as his right hand moved toward his chest where he briefly clutched a wooden cross on a necklace under his clothing.

12

Bushehr Nuclear Power Plant
Bushehr, Iran

Parsa's life had been radically changed unexpectedly just three months earlier. From the time he attended a conservative madrassah as a boy, he had faithfully observed the five tenets of Islam. He confessed that there was one God and Muhammed was his prophet. He prayed five times a day facing Mecca. He observed Ramadan and paid alms to benefit the poor. Ten years earlier he had even made the expensive pilgrimage to Mecca to march around the sacred Kaaba in the Grand Mosque.

He was thoroughly convinced that Islam was the true way. When he studied for his Ph.D. in America, a country that many of his fellow Muslims referred to as the Great Satan, some eager Christians had tried to convert him, but he had no trouble resisting them. He came back to Iran a stronger Muslim than when he left.

But then the dreams started.

Night after night he dreamed about having a conversation with a tall man with kind eyes. The dream differed each night, but usually the man approached him with his hands extended and said to him, "Parsa, Islam is not the way. I am the way."

Whenever Parsa asked the man who he was, the man just smiled a smile that warmed Parsa's heart instinctively.

"You know me as Isa, your beloved Prophet," he would say. "My name is Jesus, and I am more than a prophet. I am the Son of God. You have not followed the truth. I am the truth. And I want you to follow me."

The first night of the dream, Parsa woke up the following morning and could remember every detail. He was baffled. The next night the man appeared again. In this dream Parsa called him by the name he'd heard the night before and asked, "Jesus, why are you in my dream again?"

Jesus said, "Parsa, I love you and I want you to follow me. I can show you what real life is. I am the life."

Parsa then tried to reason with the man. "I'm Muslim. I live in a Muslim country. I can't become a Christian."

Jesus seemed undeterred. He replied, "Oh, Parsa, Parsa. I'm not talking about just changing the name of your religion. It does no good to change labels on an empty vessel. I'm calling you to follow me because I can give you a full and blessed life."

Parsa had a sense of deep tranquility and peace whenever Jesus was talking to him in the dream. These dreams continued for three weeks without interruption. He feared that he was going crazy and wondered if the stress of his job was causing him to hallucinate.

Parsa had to talk to someone—but who could he trust? He decided to talk to his older brother, Armeen, a respected physician in Tehran and devout Muslim. Armeen had never married because he was so committed to his healing profession. He asked Armeen over to their house for dinner one night that week.

After the meal, Parsa's wife, Esta, served baklava and coffee for dessert. Parsa let their nine-year-old son, Ahmed, take a piece of the sweet treat and then instructed him to give his uncle a hug goodnight.

"Go on to bed, my son," Parsa told Ahmed. "We're going to stay up and talk a little while."

Ahmed took his dessert with him and happily retreated to his bedroom. After a few more minutes of small talk, Parsa found his courage to speak honestly.

"Brother, I invited you over tonight because I have a serious problem. I respect you as my brother and as a doctor. I need help."

Esta had a look of surprise in her eyes. "Parsa," she interrupted. "Why haven't you talked to me about this problem?"

Parsa said, "I'm sorry, Esta. I didn't know who to turn to." Then he looked at his wife and brother and added, "I think I might be mentally unstable, or perhaps I have a brain tumor."

Armeen leaned forward concerned. "Please, little brother, tell me what are the symptoms you are suffering?"

Parsa paused and ate the last part of his baklava to gather his thoughts. "It's hard to explain. But I've been having...well...I've been having the same dream every night for the past month."

Silence.

Parsa began to lose his nerve and said, "It's nothing. I think I might just be stressed out because of the pressures of my job."

"And what is this dream about?" Armeen asked determinedly.

"How can I describe it?" Parsa said cautiously, realizing that he really didn't want to go forward with this conversation, but it was too late to back out. "This man appears to me in my dreams claiming that he is

Isa, one of our prophets. But in these dreams, he tells me that he is the Son of the living God and that he wants me to follow him."

Esta's eyes filled with tears as she raised a hand to her quivering lips. "Parsa," she whispered. "I've been having similar dreams, too. I was afraid to tell you."

Parsa and Esta turned to Armeen to see his reaction. They expected that he would be surprised or even outraged. Instead, a huge smile broke out on his face.

"You are not alone," he told them. "Jesus came to me in a dream three years ago. Since then, I have been a devoted follower of Jesus. I have been praying for both of you, and now my prayers have been answered."

Parsa and Esta let this news sink in as Armeen continued, "Outwardly, I still go through the rituals of Islam. But when I'm praying, I'm speaking to God in the name of Jesus. I am praying for the salvation of my family and my fellow Iranians. I still fast during Ramadan, but I'm fasting and praying for a spiritual awakening to sweep through our nation."

Parsa sat dumfounded for a moment and finally asked, "So do you still study the Quran?"

"I know the Quran almost by heart, brother," Armeen said, laughing. "But now I am a student of the true Word of God, the Bible. Every time I read it or listen to it, it's like a nourishing drink of cool water or a good meal. My soul is satisfied."

Esta was perplexed. Bibles were illegal in Iran. "How do you find one?" she wanted to know.

Armeen pulled out his smartphone and said, "It's simple. You can find the Bible in Farsi or Arabic online. There are many websites and apps that offer the Bible."

Parsa scoffed and said, "But that's impossible. Doesn't VAJA monitor websites and Internet use of all citizens?"

"You're a scientist. You do the math," Armeen countered. "Brother, there are 82 million people in Iran! How many intelligence officers would it take to monitor all the Internet use? They just use that as a scare tactic. Besides, it's possible for one to find Bible teaching on the radio and satellite television. Our government hasn't found a way to block those signals."

Parsa shook his head. This was a world he had never even heard about—and it was right in front of him all along. "So you are saying you are Christian, then?" He looked at his wife who was still trying to get her head around this amazing revelation. "I never could imagine it."

"No, I don't call myself a Christian," Armeen responded. "I'm just a follower of Isa. Don't you see, little brother? There must be several million Jesus-followers in Iran. The numbers keep growing. But, like me, they must keep it a secret—even in their own families."

Parsa was growing excited. "How do you know there are so many people in Iran following Jesus?"

Amreen smiled. "The first Christians were persecuted and killed for their faith as well. They developed a secret symbol to identify themselves to another Christian. They would draw two simple arcs that intercepted each other in the dirt." Armeen took his finger and traced two short, curved lines on the table to form the outline of a fish and its tail. He then explained how the Greek letters that spelled "fish" also formed an acrostic that stood for "Jesus is God's Son and Savior."

"So Christians in Iran draw a secret fish everywhere?" Parsa asked. "That seems strange. And I've not seen this symbol."

Amreen shook his head. "We have something better." He demonstrated by holding out his right hand as if he were going to shake someone's hand. Then he wiggled his fingers slightly as he gently moved his hand forward a few inches.

Esta laughed. "A fish!"

"We've been told this is also the practice in many Muslim countries when two Christians meet," Armeen said. "In the course of the conversation, one Christian uses the word 'fish' and then the other makes this symbol with their hand in return. Nobody would suspect anything!

"Is it safe?" Esta asked.

"It's safe to suspect they are a believer if this transpires. But it's best to keep up one's guard until you're certain."

Parsa held up his hand and waved his fingers like a fish swimming. "That's amazing. So, who told you about the fish sign?"

Amreen said, "My older partner in my medical practice. I had this same conversation with him three years ago when I was having the dreams, and he told me how to start following Jesus and how to grow as a believer. He died last year. Ordinarily I would be sad, but I know that he is enjoying Heaven with Jesus now."

Parsa grew serious. "Brother, will these dreams of Jesus keep occurring to me?"

Armeen considered this for a minute. "They may. But you don't need the dreams anymore. They stopped for me after I placed my trust in Jesus. You have something better than dreams to teach you about Isa, and that's the New Testament in the Bible. If you believe that Jesus is truly the Son of God, then you can become a part of God's family."

Parsa said, "Is that all? I just have to believe?"

Esta said firmly, "I believe Jesus is the Son of God."

Armeen grinned. "Bless you, my sister. I have been memorizing parts of the New Testament to try to learn God's Word. There's a verse that says that if you confess with your mouth that Jesus is your Lord, and believe in your heart that God raised him from the dead, you will be saved."

"Saved from what?" Parsa asked. He was not yet ready to be as bold as his wife until he had answers to some of his questions.

"You will be saved from the penalty for your sins—which is separation from God," Armeen replied, but he could see that this went right over his brother's head. So he took another approach. "You know how every year Muslims sacrifice an animal on Qurbani to make atonement for sins?"

Esta and Parsa nodded.

"We don't need to do that anymore because Jesus is the Lamb of God who takes away the sin of the world. If you are willing to confess that he is your Lord, and believe that he is God's Son, then your sins will be forgiven. That's what it means to be saved." Armeen paused. "Are you ready to make that decision?"

Parsa looked at Esta with a newfound love in his heart because she was ready to follow Jesus before he was. He nodded, "I confess that Jesus is my Lord." Parsa felt a conviction in his heart that outpaced anything he'd experienced in all his years of devotion to Islam.

Esta had tears streaming down her face. "I confess that Jesus is my Lord," she said.

"Then welcome to God's family!" Armeen said. He stood up and opened his arms. Parsa and Esta joined his embrace.

Armeen reached around his neck and removed a leather necklace he'd tucked under his shirt. At the end of the necklace was a small wooden cross. "Here. A brother gave me this when I started following Jesus, and now I want you to have it."

He placed the cross around his brother's neck, where it would remain for the rest of Parsa's days. This was the secret Parsa carried on his body every day when he went to work—a symbol of his Christian faith that could cost him his life. But now, he was willing to die for his Lord.

Parsa said, "Esta, I love you more than ever." Then he held his wife and said with a serious tone of voice, "But I want to protect you." Because of the work Parsa was involved in, he did not want his family to remain in Iran. "My work is becoming too dangerous, my love. And now we are in even greater danger because of our faith in Jesus."

Esta nodded.

"Take our son and go visit your parents in Kuwait City." Esta had dual citizenship and could come and go as she pleased. "Stay there until I can come for you."

Armeen agreed with his little brother. "Esta, I know you want to stay with Parsa. And now more than ever. But I must side with your husband. Everyone knows things are coming to a climax here in the Middle East, and we would feel safer if you weren't in Iran right now."

Parsa thought to himself how little "everyone" knew about what was really going on and how close they were to full-scale global war.

Esta wept quietly as she spoke. "I don't want to leave any of you. But if that's what you insist, I will make plans to visit my parents."

13

The Office of the Supreme Leader
Central Tehran
The Islamic Republic of Iran

Ayatollah Sayyid Ali Mazdaki had convened an emergency meeting of his top government officials to respond to the growing crisis in Israel. These men were seated on the floor while Mazdaki towered above them to demonstrate his absolute authority. He was trying to stay calm on the outside, but inside he was boiling with anger.

On paper, Iran appears to have a complex government structure. For most of its history, the nation was known as Persia and was ruled for many generations by a dictator who was considered a king and was later called Shah. This changed in 1978 with the revolution and overthrow of Shah Mohammed Reza Pahlavi. Since then, Iran had been led by two Supreme Leaders. First, Ruhollah Khamenei held the position until his death in 1989. At his death the Assembly of Experts, a collection of respected Islamic Imams, chose Savyid Ali Mazdaki as Supreme Leader.

Iran has a constitution, adopted by referendum, and upholds a separation of powers model with Executive, Legislative, and Judicial branches. The citizens elect a president. There is also a Speaker of Parliament and a Chief Justice. In reality, however, Iran is a theocracy, and the Supreme Leader is the absolute governmental and religious authority. As such, Mazdaki served as Commander-in-Chief of the military and routinely fired and appointed cabinet members at his sole discretion. He chose which candidates could run for office—and which ones were to remain silent.

The room was hushed, waiting for the Supreme Leader to speak. The silence lingered until everyone was uncomfortable. But the Ayatollah continued to stare them down.

He raised his hand to impose silence. His words were clipped as he growled in Farsi, "What fool among you dared to tell me that this military exercise against occupied Palestine wouldn't result in any casualties?"

Some of the men looked around to see if anyone volunteered to respond.

He continued, "And which of you have camel dung for brains and insisted that these so-called small explosions couldn't even be traced back to our government?"

After another few moments of smothering silence, President Turin Abassi spoke up. "Your Excellency, we didn't anticipate that the Great Satan, the Americans, would have the advanced satellite surveillance to track the origin of our missiles. And as to the deaths of the pilots over Palestine, well, they could be considered a random case of pilot error."

Mazdaki's lips curled in a snarl. "That is idiotic logic, Mr. President. The Jews have the digital readout of the time of the collision of the jets, and it happened seconds after your EMP missiles exploded. Perhaps you know the saying from the desert, 'When you ride a camel, you can't crouch.' And you're not going to be able to hide behind your advisors this time. I should have stepped in and cancelled the launch, but I didn't. So, there will be consequences for you."

President Abassi's face grew pale. "But Your Excellency, I would humbly remind you that this action was your idea, and we were only pleased to support your decision."

The rest of the men shifted their body weight uncomfortably. Abassi was in real danger of incurring the wrath of the Supreme Leader at any moment. The president took his cues and decided not to go farther down that road. He cleared his throat. "But you're right, there will be consequences. We have placed our military on alert. We are expecting a full-scale military strike in reprisal."

Mazdaki was clearly irritated and bit off each word. "Mr. President, you signed off on the attack. And now, you will accompany my generals to lead a frontline command center to prepare for the defense of our nation."

The Ayatollah looked through the assembled men until his eyes found Parsa Turan. "Dr. Turan, I want you to stay for a few minutes after everyone leaves." He waved his hand in a dismissal. "The rest of you can leave now!"

The leaders jumped to their feet and hurried out of the room like leaves being blown by a whirlwind. The Ayatollah motioned for Parsa to approach his seat.

Parsa began perspiring immediately. He slowly shuffled toward the Supreme Leader. He feared that somehow his secret about his recent conversion had been reported. He knew that information would carry a death sentence in Iran. He prayed silently, *"Lord, please give me your help."*

Mazdaki stared at him coldly until the room cleared.

"Dr. Turan, what is the status of your special assignment?"

Inwardly, Parsa breathed a silent prayer of thanks. He knew that the development of nuclear warheads was only known to the Supreme Leader and a few trusted aids. To everyone else it was just an unnamed special assignment.

Mazdaki became impatient with Parsa's silence and demanded, "Well, report something! How soon will the project be completed?"

Parsa looked humbly at his boss and groveled, "I'm sorry, Your Excellency. The process of enrichment cannot be rushed. We are still several weeks away from completion."

Mazdaki glared at Parsa. "What if I told you that you don't have several weeks? What else do you need to complete the task?"

"Only time. Over the past six months, we have been working to enrich the uranium ore that the Russians provided us. It's a long process to convert uranium to enriched uranium 235. Nuclear fission can only occur with uranium 235 or plutonium 239. If we had plutonium we would be ready, but the Russians or the Chinese weren't willing to provide us with plutonium."

Mazdaki held up his hand. "Please don't bore me with that scientific gibberish. Tell me how long it will take for the weapons to be ready."

Parsa consulted his tablet and swiped to find

the correct chart. "We currently have about 4,000 centrifuges operating to convert the uranium oxide into the chemical uranium hexafluoride. At this rate, we will have enough enriched uranium in twelve days."

"Good. And how many warheads will that allow us to create?"

Parsa hesitated. "Just one, sir. That was all I was told to build."

The Ayatollah stood up and turned to leave. "One is all we need to destroy the Jewish pigs. You have twelve days and not a minute longer." Then he looked thoughtfully at the scientist and added, "You know, what we are doing will fulfill the prophecy for the return of the Twelfth Imam."

"Yes, Your Excellency," Parsa said, but inside he was thinking, *I used to believe the Twelver theology too. But now I know the truth. I realize that it's all a lie.*

The Ayatollah stopped and spoke again, "Dr. Turan, if you don't have that bomb ready in twelve days, I will have your head, literally. I am bringing a new enforcer to carry out my wishes."

Parsa was dismissed and walked toward the rear exit. When he reached the hallway he stopped to lean against the wall. His heart was heaving, and Parsa wondered for a minute if he might have a stroke.

He closed his eyes and silently prayed, *"God, there's no way the bomb will be ready in that time. Besides, Lord, now I can't build a weapon to kill millions of people. Help me figure out a way to stop this crazy plan to destroy Israel. Please send me someone who can help me. I'm desperate, Lord. I'm asking on behalf of your Son, Jesus. Amen."*

14

The Kremlin
Moscow, Russia

Russian President Mikhail Sokolov sat at the head of a modern conference table inside the Presidential Building in the Kremlin. He was flanked by his appointed Prime Minister, Benjamin Yukavits, and his Minister of Defense, Sergey Novakova. They were looking at a large monitor on the wall with an image of the Iranian Ayatollah Mazdaki speaking.

Formal relations between Russia and Iran had a long history, beginning in 1521 with a treaty between the Russian Czar Vasilli III and the Persian Shah Ismail I. The relationship between the two countries was long and complex—sometimes as allies and often as rivals. Currently, it had never been stronger. Due to severe Western economic sanctions against Iran, Russia has become their chief trading partner. Russia purchased excess oil from Iran, and Iran purchased weapons from Russia. Two years ago, Russia and Iran had signed an oil-for-goods deal worth twenty billion dollars. Without Russia, Iran's economy would have collapsed.

Russian President Sokolov had progressed through the ranks of the KGB before grabbing a stranglehold on the leadership of the Russian government. Sokolov was a tough-as-nails leader who successfully hid his violent temper behind a disarming smile. He had led Russia from the economic doldrums back to prominence as a world power. But he concealed a burning jealousy regarding U.S. advancements in warfare technology. In retaliation, he had launched cyber campaigns to disrupt the free elections in twenty-seven countries, including America.

"President Sokolov," Mazdaki began, "our optimistic plan to have weapons-grade uranium ready by this point was premature. Now it appears as if we are several weeks, or months, away from that point. So I am appealing to you as our global partner. We can easily increase our crude oil deliveries to Russia. But I would like to discuss the purchase of one or several of your Zircon hypersonic missiles."

President Sokolov was silent as he contemplated the offer. Finally he spoke up, "Your Excellency, why would you need our Zircon missiles?"

"We are anticipating a large-scale attack from the Zionists in response to an incident involving the EMP attack on their communications systems. As you know, they are blaming Iran. But we have evidence that the Hezbollah in Lebanon are behind this and other attacks. We only wish to defend our interests."

Sokolov replied, "Your Excellency, you are aware that international treaties prevent Russia from selling nuclear devices to another nation. By breaking these treaties we would open ourselves up to pressure from China and the United States. It's too much of a risk for us to take."

On the screen, Mazdaki's expression changed to one of irritation. "Mr. President, you are going to leave Iran defenseless in the face of an attack from the Zionists or the Americans?"

Sokolov shook his head. "Of course not. As your ally, Russia stands ready to come to your aid if any nation brings a pre-emptive strike against you. I will instruct General Novakova to maintain constant surveillance of the situation between Israel and Iran."

The Russian leader spent the next few minutes assuring Mazdaki that the Russian Bear and the Lion of Iran would continue to form a substantial force that no army on the globe would want to threaten. Mazdaki seemed pacified before they ended the call.

When the video screen went dark, President

Sokolov turned and said, "General Novakova, you know I don't care about Israel. But this may be an opportunity to strike a blow against the Americans and make it appear as if Iran is the protagonist. What do you think?"

"Mr. President, it would be difficult for us to hide our involvement in any action against Israel or the United States. The Americans' satellite surveillance net can detect the motion of a cat in a back alley of the Kremlin. We can't officially deliver the Zircon missiles to Iran, but if we could smuggle in a few through the back door, it would allow us to deny any launch from Russia."

"Do the Iranians have the equipment to launch the Zircon? It's a sea-based missile, is it not?"

Novakova nodded. "We have recently upgraded the Zircon so it can be land-based as well. It's a formidable weapon. It uses plasma stealth to avoid radar detection, and it flies at hypersonic speeds to strike quickly. It's a top-secret weapon, and I'm surprised that Mazdaki even knew about it."

Sokolov had wondered the same thing. "He is a shrewd operator, for certain. And he has a violent temper. But we may be able to manipulate him for our purposes. Bring me an operative plan to consider delivering two Zircons to him."

"Yes, Mr. President," the general said and he and

Prime Minister Yukamits left the conference room.

Sokolov spun his chair around to look out the large window overlooking Red Square. The onion domes of the St. Basil's Cathedral shone with the reflection of the setting sun. A smile creased his face as he considered the opportunities before him. If he could get Iran and America fighting each other, both countries would be at risk. Russia could then stand on the sidelines and watch as both suffered great losses. Neither President Turner nor the Ayatollah would ever win a chess game against him. The White Queen would take the Black Knight. Checkmate.

15

Highway 1 Westbound
Jerusalem to Tel Aviv

Solly, Regan, and Ty had slept a little later to avoid the worst of the rush hour traffic between Israel's two main cities, Jerusalem and Tel Aviv. They were on their way to Tel Aviv to *Mossad* headquarters for a briefing.

As they drove, they listened to all the Israeli news stations reporting the mysterious shutdown of the cellular grid and the Israeli GPS. However, though they may have suspected it, none of the news outlets reported the source of the shutdown to be Iran. The other lead story was the death of two Israeli Air Force pilots due to a midair collision.

Ty said, "It's pretty amazing to me that the press hasn't reported that Iran was the source of both events—the shutdown and the crash of the two fighter jets. They have to put them at the top of the list of culprits."

"When the Prime Minister's office wants to keep something hidden, he can generally count on the press not dig too deeply," Solly explained. "The Israeli press representatives realize we are always on a war footing with our enemies, so they consider themselves part of our wartime strategy."

"That's way different than back home," Regan noted. She was checking her phone in the backseat. Then she turned to Solly and said, "So do you have any idea what the response will be to Iran?"

Solly shook his head. "I've learned from painful experience not to try to predict what kind of retaliation will be planned. I suspect that it will be directed toward the Supreme Leader, Ayatollah Mazdaki. He is a rabid Twelver."

Regan was baffled. "What's a Twelver? I've heard that before, but I have no idea what it means."

"Do you want the short answer or the long answer?"

"I want the full answer, I think."

"Sure. But first you'd better put your phone away because there will be a test on this when we reach the main office." Solly often wished young people paid more attention to their surroundings than their phones.

He composed his thoughts and shifted to a more comfortable driving position. "Okay, mates, in order to tell you about the Twelvers you've first got to know the difference between Sunni and Shia Muslims. Do you understand that?"

Ty said, "I know that the Sunnis are in Saudi and Jordan and that Shiites are mostly in Iran and Iraq. But I don't really know what makes them different. I get the idea that they don't get along."

"That's an understatement," Solly said. "Sunnis and Shiites have killed more Muslims in terrorist attacks the last twenty years than against any other global target."

Regan said, "So which group is larger?"

"Good question. Sunni Muslims make up about 85% of all Muslims. Of the 15% of Shiites, the vast majority of them are also Twelvers."

"How long have there been two Muslim factions?" Ty asked.

"It really dates all the way back to the death of Muhammed in 632 C.E. The split occurred over a disagreement about who should be the next leader of Islam. Some argued that the leader should be part of Muhammed's family—particularly his son-in-law and cousin Ali. The other side disagreed and said the leader should be chosen by a consensus of the top Imams. The ones wanting a family member were later called *Shias*, which is a contraction of *'Shiat Ali'* which means 'follower of Ali.' The word *Sunni* comes from an Arabic word for 'traditional law.'"

"How do you know so much about this?" Regan wanted to know.

Solly smiled. "When you are a tiny nation surrounded by angry Muslims, you learn as much as you can about your enemies. Also, I gave a briefing paper on this to the Prime Minister early in my career."

"So who won the argument over the successor for Muhammed?" Ty asked.

"Well, the Sunnis won that battle. The majority voted on Abu Bakr, who was one of Muhammed's generals, but he wasn't a family member."

"Did that settle the dispute?" Regan asked.

"Not in the least. It only poured gasoline on the fire. Those who became Shiites didn't recognize Abu Bakr. After serving only two years, he died. His two elected successors were both quickly assassinated by a group who finally succeeded in getting Ali appointed as Caliph which comes from the Arabic word '*khalifa*' which means '*successor*', you see."

"So then was everybody happy?" Ty asked.

Solly shook his head as he checked his rearview mirror for traffic. "They've never been happy. The two factions continued to fight." Solly took nearly the entire rest of the trip to explain several centuries of Iranian history, including a fascinating story about how after serving as Caliph for six years, Ali was assassinated while praying in a mosque. A Sunni struck him in the head with a poisoned sword, and he died two days later. His followers were able to name his sons as the next two Caliphs. But then came the massacre at Karbala.

Solly explained that the Shiite Muslims commemorate this tragedy every year called the Day of Ashura from the year 690. Warriors of the Sunni faction herded Ali's sons and family members into a compound in Karbala. Then they proceeded to behead all of them.

"Every year Shiites mourn this day with a solemn parade," Solly added. "Many men take chains and strike themselves on their backs and cut themselves with knifes. It's really scary stuff."

Regan said, "I've seen videos of that tradition. It's awful. So the Sunnis don't do that? Only Shiites?"

Solly said, "Right. Over the centuries there have been different Caliphs elected by the religious leaders. The Shiites have only recognized two early ones. After centuries of Sunni Caliphs, the Ottoman Caliphate was dissolved 1923 by the Turkey National Assembly. So there hasn't been a Caliphate until our friend al-Bagahdi declared ISIS to be the next Caliphate."

"I thought you were going to explain something about Twelvers, but you've chased another rabbit out of the woodpile like usual," Regan teased. The thing about Solly was there was always so much he could teach you about anything—and he knew how to keep your attention.

Solly laughed, "No, my dear. There really are two rabbits—Sunni and Shiite. I'm getting there. You need to know that no Sunnis are Twelvers, but about 80% of Shiites are Twelvers. And Iran is the only country where Twelver Islam is the official state religion. So now I'm ready to give you the shorter answer to the Twelver question."

Regan checked her watch and noticed they were already in Tel Aviv by this point. "Well it's about time," she joked.

"Alright, you'll just have to listen quicker then," Solly said. He went on to explain how Twelvers believe that there were twelve special Imams appointed by Allah, and they were all descendants of Muhammed. The last, or Twelfth Imam was a boy in Iraq who was hidden by Allah in the ninth century. His name was Muhammed al-Mahdi. Twelvers, Solly explained, believe that the Mahdi will return or be revealed at the climax of history to become the world leader—like a Messiah. Shiite Twelvers also believe that the Mahdi's return will coincide with the return of Jesus Christ.

"They believe that Jesus will assist the Mahdi in a fight against a wicked world ruler—like the Antichrist," Solly added.

"You're kidding!" Ty interjected. "They actually believe that Jesus is coming back?"

Solly put on the turn signal to turn into the Mossad Central Office parking deck.

"I thought you were asleep by now, Ty! Good boy! Why, yes. They believe that Jesus, or Isa, was born of a virgin and lived a sinless life. They don't believe the biblical account that Jesus was crucified or resurrected. Instead, they think he was taken to Paradise and will one day return. But, when he does return, they think he'll be the assistant Messiah to the Twelfth Imam. They teach that Jesus will proclaim Islam as the true religion, and all Christians will convert. All other religions will be erased. All crosses will be broken, and all the pigs...Jews...will be exterminated. So you can see that the Twelvers have it all planned out."

"That's some plan," Ty remarked as Solly parked the Range Rover in a space that had a temporary sign with Solly's name on it.

"Yes," Solly said and turned the engine off. "So you see that's what we're up against. Let's go find out what the boss has planned for us."

16

Mossad Headquarters
Tel Aviv, Israel

"The Director will see you now," the administrative assistant announced to Solly, Ty, and Regan. They had been sitting silently in her office for almost forty-five minutes beyond their scheduled appointment time. Ty and Regan worked on their phones catching up with texts and emails, while Solly had pulled his Stetson over his nose to take a power nap.

As Solly entered the entered the office of *Mossad* Director Asher Hazzan, followed by Ty and Regan, he saw Ziv Kessler, advisor to Prime Minister Natan Abrams, seated on the couch smoking a cigarette. Ziv was a heavy smoker, and Solly waved his hand, batting at the air dramatically as he approached Kessler. "Haven't you guys heard of the Clean Air act, global warming and all that?" he asked.

Ziv took a final puff and crushed out the cigarette

in an ash tray. "Yeah," he said in a gruff voice, "I figure the planet is going to become uninhabitable in about four thousand years."

"At this rate," Asher said, "We're going to kill off everyone a lot sooner than that."

"Now, there's an idea. Let's start by killing off the Iranians," Ziv said.

Regan sat down in one of the chairs facing the couch. "Surely, you don't mean that, do you?"

Ziv smiled at the American, stood, and shook everyone's hands. They hadn't seen each other since last year when Solly, Ty, and Regan had thwarted a terrorist plot to destroy Jerusalem.

"I absolutely mean that," Ziv deadpanned. "If the Iranians could kill every Jew, they would do it in a heartbeat."

"In less than a heartbeat," Asher added. "After that EMP attack yesterday, we have to accelerate our strategy to disable or disarm them. Ziv and I have been working on a plan to do just that."

Solly said, "I gather that's why we're here."

Asher shook his head. "That's why *you're* here, Solly. We didn't invite Ty and Regan to this meeting. Only you. As an agent for *Mossad* we expect you to take risks, not civilians."

He then turned to Regan and Ty. "No offense intended, but we don't want to involve you in this project since you're American citizens. We'd like to ask you to step out into the waiting area while we discuss strategy with Solly."

Regan, who had a lifelong problem taking "no" for an answer, was not so easily dissuaded. "We're not Jews, and we're not Israelis, that's true," she began. "But Ty and I have both risked our lives for Israel. You'll recall I was kidnapped and held hostage in Gaza because I was helping Israel. You remember we both risked being burned to a crisp by a nuclear device because we love Israel. You don't have to pay us a nickel, but we're here to help Solly." She turned to Ty and demanded, "Right, Ty?"

Ty, who had been thinking about how close he and Regan had come to death since their meeting, was suddenly startled into replying. "Uh, absolutely, Regan. We are here to help."

There was silence for a few minutes while everyone allowed the tense atmosphere to subside.

Regan was not nearly finished. "There is a Latin saying on the back of a U.S. dollar bill. It's one of two mottos on the Great Seal of the United States. The motto is '*Annuit Coeptis*.' Do you know what that Latin phrase means?"

"Of course," Ziv said. "It means 'He (God) has favored our endeavors.' I believe it was chosen by your Founding Fathers to acknowledge God's blessing on their fight for freedom."

Regan pointed to Ty and Solly and said, "That's right. And when it comes to the three of us working together, I would say, '*Annuit Coeptis.*' God has favored our endeavors as a team."

Solly decided to interject and give Regan a breather. "Director Hazzan, Regan is right. We are a team. I wouldn't be here today, and I daresay none of us would be here today if it wasn't for this team. God has blessed us. I say we stick together."

"Right!" Regan and Ty said simultaneously.

Asher looked at Ziv, who sighed and nodded with an attitude of resignation. "Okay," Asher said. "But this mission is more dangerous than anything you've attempted before."

Ty and Regan nodded eagerly. It sounded exciting.

"You may or may not know that Asher was a part of the commandos who stormed Entebbe when he was a young man," Ziv began. "We were talking about that operation just now and about how crucial subterfuge was to the mission. Without our soldiers impersonating Idi Amin, it would not have worked."

Ty said, "So we're going to impersonate a dead African dictator?"

Asher laughed at the joke.

"No," Ziv continued. "You're going to impersonate

inspectors from the INRC, the International Nuclear Regulatory Commission. Iran routinely allows these United Nations inspection teams to visit their facilities as part of their treaty with the European Union. These teams are usually comprised of three inspectors and a technician. We were planning on sending Solly as a representative from Bahrain, which is a Shiite majority nation, because Solly speaks fluent Arabic."

Ty shot a look of surprise over at Solly. In all the years he'd known his friend, he never knew he was fluent in Arabic. Solly just grinned and wiggled his thick eyebrows up and down.

"We were planning to send two other *Mossad* agents with him," Ziv offered. "But now we need to adjust the plans."

"Ziv, I speak French like a Parisian from the decade that I worked there for my Investment Company," Regan said. She looked at Ty. "Who can you be?" she asked incredulously.

"Well, I speak Texan. But I guess that won't work."

"Not for that reason. It's that Iran will not allow American inspectors since President Turner withdrew from the treaty last year," Asher explained.

Ty thought for a moment and replied, "Well, I suppose I could be Canadian. I've been to the Calgary stampede. How's this?" Ty, in a heavy Canadian accent, said, "I'm aboot to go to the rodeo. You betcha, aye?"

Regan laughed and said, "That's awful! I think you should stay quiet and nod."

"I can do that."

"Okay," Asher said. "We'll work on it. Mission briefing begins this afternoon at 14:00."

"Can you give us an idea of the mission objective?" Solly asked.

"The EMP attack by Iran poked a sharp stick in the eye of Israel," Ziv explained. "It was designed to provoke us into a large-scale retaliation. They will be expecting a huge military response. But I'm betting on the old saying that 'you don't need a sledgehammer to crack a nut.' While Iran is expecting the sledgehammer, we're going to slip into their house and steal the nut."

Ty shook his head. "I don't get what you're saying. Who or what is the nut?"

Asher looked at Ziv and nodded his approval.

"You're going to kidnap the head of the Iranian Nuclear Agency, Dr. Parsa Turan," Ziv said. "Our intelligence sources tell us Dr. Parsa is the brains behind the enrichment of the uranium required to manufacture a nuclear warhead. If he is out of the picture, their progress comes to a dead halt."

There was a moment of stunned silence. Finally Solly looked at Ty and Regan and said, "Oh, no problem, mates. So we're going inside Iran to kidnap a nuclear scientist. I thought we were going to be assigned a *really* hard mission."

Solly had always liked the motto of the U.S. Corps of Engineers. *"The difficult we do immediately. The impossible will take a little longer."*

And a little longer was all they had to keep the Iranians from launching a nuclear war.

17

Mossad Headquarters
Tel Aviv, Israel

At 14:00, Solly, Ty, and Regan reconvened for the next step in the mission briefing. They were to meet with Professor Ehud Silverman, the Guggenheim Endowed Professor of Islamic Studies at the Hebrew University in Jerusalem. Dr. Silverman was *Mossad's* foremost expert on Islamic eschatology. A graduate of Stanford and Oxford University, he had published more academic articles on Islamic eschatology than anyone else in the world. What was less well known about Dr. Silverman was that he was also an expert on Israeli ordinance, an interest he called his personal hobby.

To their surprise, Dr. Silverman turned out to be a thirty-something hipster with hair long enough to cascade onto his thick shoulders. His scraggly beard matched the color of his baggy shorts, and he sported a loose-fitting retro t-shirt emblazoned with the face of Bob Marley. Birkenstock sandals completed his academic regalia.

Director Asher Hazzan made introductions. "Dr. Silverman is here to brief us on some key background information to inform our mission. Iran, as you know, is committed to wiping out Israel—and the United States. But it's a mistake to think they are driven to madness solely because of the Jews. There is a theological motivation behind their acts that is crucial to the execution of our mission. Today he'll give you a short course behind Iran's belief that they can bring on the return of the Mahdi and usher in the end of time by attacking Israel."

Ty, Regan, and Solly sat around a conference table adjoining Asher's office. They had been given iPads pre-loaded with the outline of Dr. Silverman's presentation. Ty fumbled with his iPad and whispered to Solly, "I was expecting more of a weapons orientation than a college lecture."

Solly winked at Ty and said to Dr. Silverman, "On our drive over from Jerusalem I gave Ty and Regan a short explanation of what the Twelvers believe about Jesus and the Mahdi. So, we're a little ahead of the game."

"Good. That will save me some of my lecture," Dr. Silverman said. "So let's get started. Swipe down on your iPads to see what I'm going to be talking about."

The three teammates looked at their iPads as instructed. Ty noticed that there were 64 slides to the presentation. He sighed and settled deeper into his thick leather office chair.

Dr. Silverman began with identifying the two important holy scriptures for Muslims: the Quran and the Hadith. The Quran, he explained, contains supposed statements that God gave to Muhammed through the angel Gabriel. Muhammed was illiterate, so he was unable to write down any of these sayings. So there were scribes who wrote down what Muhammed claimed God said to him over a twenty-three-year period until his death in 632 C.E. These sayings were compiled by the scribes after Muhammed died. The Quran is roughly the length of the Christian New Testament and is made up of 114 surahs, or chapters.

The Quran, Dr. Silverman pointed out, has no teaching about eschatology or last things. Only the Hadith, a collection of sayings attributed to Muhammed that are not considered to be direct revelations from God.

"The Hadith also contains stories about what Muhammed did, like his journey from Jerusalem to the seventh heaven," Dr. Silverman added.

Regan's ears perked up. "I remember we learned about that from Dr. David Shvaz at the Temple Institute in Jerusalem last year."

Dr. Silverman smiled. "That's wonderful that you are already familiar with the Hadith. Do all of you know then about the predictions about the end of time?"

Solly said, "No, I don't think we've been briefed on that yet."

"Excellent," Dr. Silverman said and began his lecture again. They learned that the Hadith was not organized until two hundred years after Muhammed's death and burial in Medina. A scholar by the name of al-Bukhari collected a total of 600,000 alleged sayings from Muhammed. These came from the writings of Muhammed's friends and family members. Many of them came from Muhammed's 15 wives.

"Of these sayings, al-Bukhari verified that 7,000 of them were genuine, and so they were included in the Hadith," Dr. Silverman said.

Ty asked, "Okay, but what verification process did he use to choose some sayings and reject others? Sounds willy nilly to me."

Dr. Silverman replied, "That's a good question. No Islamic scholar can answer that. Perhaps some just felt right, and others felt wrong. Nobody knows. When you take the time to read the entire Hadith in Arabic, as I have, there are actually some bizarre sayings attributed to Muhammed. Regan, I warn you, you're not going to like some of them."

Regan narrowed her eyes.

Dr. Silverman referred them to their iPads where he had listed various sayings, including the surah and verse references. According to the Hadith, Muhammed said:

"Women are deficient in mind." (2:541 and 3:826)

"The majority of people in hell are women." (1:28, 301; 2:161; 7:124)

"Drinking camel urine will make you healthy." (7:590)

"Though I am an apostle of Allah, yet I do not know what Allah will do to me." (2:375)

"If you speak badly about a deceased person, that person will go to hell." (2:448)

Solly ran his eyes over these phrases. "Oh, boy. I've read the Quran, but I never knew those sayings were in the Hadith."

"Anyone can look them up and verify them," Dr. Silverman said. "Among Muslims today, they consider the Hadith to be just as binding as the Quran. There is a very complex system explained for the afterlife in the Hadith. If you know about Muhammed's questionable journey to Allah, you're familiar with the seven levels of Paradise."

Dr. Silverman went on to explain that, according to the Hadith, there are seven levels of hell as well. The first level is the purgatorial level that some Muslims who were not quite faithful will have to pass through. "That may be the source of the Roman Catholic doctrine of purgatory," the professor suggested. "The Hadith teaches that Christians are assigned to the second level of hell. The third level of hell is for the Jews. Level four is for the Sabeans. The fifth level is for the Zoroastrians, which was the predominate religion of Persia before Islam. Level six is for idolaters and level seven is for hypocrites. Humans will be punished in hell by demons. This torture will continue eternally. It's quite an elaborate system."

Ty looked up. "And all of this is in the Hadith? It sounds crazy."

"Yes. I told you there are many, many teachings in the Hadith. I mentioned earlier that there are no end time predictions in the Quran. But there are plenty of end time signs that point to a climatic event in Islamic eschatology. It's called 'The Hour' in the Hadith."

Regan, Solly, and Ty listened spellbound as Dr. Silverman continued his presentation. The parallels between Islam and Christianity were astounding.

"It's important to remember," Dr. Silverman explained, "that although Muhammed was illiterate, he had heard the teachings of both the Old and New Testaments of the Bible. In Islam, the Hadith says that only God knows the exact timing of the 'the hour.' That sounds similar to what Jesus said about no one knowing the day or the hour, only the Father."

"So you know the New Testament as well as

Islamic theology?" Regan asked,

"Of course. I consider myself a completed Jew. I can read the Bible in the original languages of Hebrew, Aramaic, and Greek. When I was in my early twenties studying at Oxford University, I wrote an essay comparing the Old Testament prophecies about the Messiah to the actions and statements of the Jewish rabbi, Jesus. Through that process, I came to be convinced that Jesus of Nazareth is the Messiah. I'm connected with a large group of Messianic Jews who fellowship together in the Old City of Jerusalem."

Solly slapped the table with his hand and pointed at the professor. "I knew there was something about you I liked! I'm just like you." Dr. Silverman and Solly exchanged a knowing grin.

"Why then is Iran attacking Israel? It's simple," the professor continued. "Although the Mahdi is not mentioned in the Quran, Shiites insist that his existence is inferred. In the belief of Twelvers, including the current Supreme Leader of Iran, warfare with Israel and her allies will usher in the return of the Mahdi."

He explained that it is the Mahdi who will take the place of the New Testament predictions about Jesus. Similar to Jesus, the Mahdi will defeat the Antichrist and create a kingdom that will fill the earth with goodness and justice. He is the one who has been destined from eternity to save the world from the forces of wickedness. In Shiite eschatology, Jesus is limited to helping the Mahdi propagate Islam among the Christians and Jews.

Ty was paying attention now. "So, all of this political and military maneuvering is based upon the religious beliefs of the Iranians?"

Asher interjected, "That's right. I thought it was imperative that you guys understand what's going on in the mind of Ayatollah Mazdaki. He doesn't just hate Israel. He truly believes that by drawing us into a war, he is ushering in the Second Coming. Therefore, he is desperate to produce a nuclear weapon to destroy Israel. Our intelligence reports that it is only a matter of time."

Asher turned and thanked Dr. Silverman and informed Solly, Ty, and Regan about the rest of the day's agenda. "The next stop for you three is to assume your new identities," he explained. "Israel may be as far removed from Hollywood as you can get, but our guys can perform miracles when it comes to disguises." Asher paused and shot Solly a playful look.

"You like that beard, Sol?" Solly stroked his beard instinctively and nodded, a worried look on his face. "Well that's too bad," Asher joked.

They made plans to meet later that evening at Ramat David Airbase for a final briefing.

18

Ramat David Air Force Base
Jezreel Valley, Israel

Ramat David Air Force base, one of the three principle airbases of the Israeli Air Force, is located in the plain of the Jezreel Valley close to Megiddo. This is the biblical location of Armageddon. The base is named after a nearby kibbutz, one of many communal Jewish settlements throughout Israel. In an impressive show of strength, Israeli aircraft routinely take off and land on the surface of the base's three runways that form a large triangle. When not on patrol, the fighter jets are safely hidden from aerial attack in underground hangars beneath the runways. The planes launch using an ingenious catapult system modeled after the systems used on U.S. aircraft carriers, sending multiple warplanes into the sky like angry hornets.

Solly, Ty, and Regan arrived at Ramat David via helicopter for their briefing, which was to take place below ground in one of the massive hangars. Once they were escorted inside, they saw their ride awaiting them: a white jet with the United Nations logo featured on the fuselage and tail. Ty immediately recognized the EMJ 145, a twin-engine regional jet produced by Embraer, a Brazilian aerospace company. The aircraft can accommodate up to 50 passengers, but on this flight, there would be a flight crew of only two persons, along with passengers Solly, Ty, and Regan who would pose as members of the International Nuclear Regulatory Commission. Four large seats filled the front of the passenger cabin, the remaining seats having been removed to carry necessary equipment. Solly wondered who belonged in the extra seat.

Two Israeli Air Force pilots dressed as U.N. pilots with forged credentials were planning to fly the group first to Vienna, Austria, the location of the European office of the INRC. There they would file a flight plan to Tehran, the capital of Iran. Israeli computer experts had already hacked the INRC system and entered fictitious names of all the players and scheduled flights. In the unexpected event that Iranian officials tried to verify their identities, these same hackers had broken into international record systems to add the names and backgrounds of all the imposters.

Before the briefing, Solly, Ty, and Regan were

escorted to a changing area where they underwent makeovers to suit their new identities. Solly returned dressed in the traditional Arab dress of a long, white robe called a *thobe*. The top was tailored like a shirt, but the bottom was loose to his ankle. He wore the traditional *ghutra*, or rectangular headscarf worn by men with a rope band around it called an *egal*. Over his *thobe* he wore a dark brown cloak called a *bisht*, typically worn by high-level government officials on special occasions.

A walking stick with a gold-encrusted handle completed the disguise, the distinctive accessory of many wealthy Arabs. To his relief, Solly's full beard was safely deemed appropriate for a respected Muslim businessman. His passport (pre-stamped with visas from Muslim-majority countries) identified him as Nabil Samar, a nuclear scientist from the small kingdom of Bahrain. Solly slipped effortlessly into his character and began addressing everyone in Arabic.

Regan appeared next, dressed as a modern European female Muslim professional. She wore an *abaya*, a stylish long dress that reached to her ankles. The outer material was dark gray, but the undergarment that covered her arms was a brilliant red to match the *hijab* covering her hair. Her shoes and purse were matching Gucci black Sylvie in crocodile, and her nails and make up were perfection. Her

French passport identified her as Dr. Noor Jamila. She quickly memorized her cover story—a native of Kuwait who had lived in France for ten years working as a journalist for a scientific magazine.

Ty's passport identified him as Dr. Oscar Williams, a physics professor at the University of Calgary in Alberta. His transformation was less elaborate than the others, and he donned an inexpensive button-down shirt and khakis that a middle-aged college academic might wear.

"Great. I'm dressed as a nerd," Ty complained to Regan, who tried not to laugh.

"You *are* a nerd, Ty," she teased him.

As the almost unrecognizable trio waited for the meeting to begin, they soon learned the identity of the fourth passenger who would accompany them. Regan caught herself staring when Sven Johannessen, a *Mossad* agent, walked into the room and introduced himself.

He stood a little over six feet tall and had a thick mane of blonde hair. His deep-set eyes were the deep blue shade of a glacier. Sven had the rugged good looks of a Nordic skier who had spent much of his life outdoors.

Asher called the meeting to order as all the operatives sat around a table next to the parked jet. He gave Solly, Ty, and Regan a brief overview of their new teammate. Sven, they learned, was one of the most celebrated Nordic skiers in Sweden with two Olympic gold medals. Sven's mother was Jewish, and he had immigrated to Israel after his Olympic career to study physics. Once in Israel he had been enlisted by *Mossad* as an information officer. During field training, Sven learned Farsi and had spent the past year translating intercepted radio transmissions from Iran.

Asher had tapped Sven to serve as the inspection team technician during this mission. Sven had been training around the clock with Israeli nuclear scientists digesting the fundamentals necessary for an authentic inspection. Their teammate was wearing the uniform of a United Nations colonel, and his Swedish passport identified him as a nuclear engineer employed by the United Nations.

Asher next moved to the goals and objectives of their assignment. "This mission is fraught with risks and uncertainties," he said. "It's not the first time we have entered a sovereign nation to carry out an operation. However, our normal *modus operandi* is to slip in, make a kill, and then slip out undetected. Our agency has kidnapped individuals, including former Nazis who have been hiding from justice. However, we have never attempted to capture an Iranian citizen until now."

Asher continued, "The plan is simple but dangerous. You will fly from here to Vienna at a very low altitude without filing a flight plan. The flight will take about four hours. Once on the ground, you'll refuel. Our pilots will then file an official United Nations flight plan to Bushehr International Airport in Iran. Dr. Turan will meet you there and escort you to the Bushehr Nuclear Power Plant located near the Persian Gulf. We believe this is where the illegal enrichment of weapons-grade uranium is underway."

Satellite surveillance had showed eight Series 2-300 Russian-made anti-aircraft missile systems installed near Bushehr and guarded continually by dozens of soldiers from the Republican Guard armed with MPT-9 submachine guns. These Iranian copies of the Heckler & Koch MP-5 carried 15-round magazines and were extremely capable weapons. Asher believed armed members of VAJA would be present as well.

"Are there any questions so far?" the director wanted to know.

Ty asked, "Will we have any weapons?"

Asher shook his head. "You will be searched upon arrival. Inspection teams are never armed." He paused. "Actually, you will have one weapon. Twist the handle of your walking stick, Solly."

Solly twisted the head of the walking stick and

revealed a hidden razor sharp eight-inch stiletto. "At least it's something," Solly commented. "But don't you know that you should never take a knife to a gun fight?"

Ty laughed.

Asher ignored this and continued, "One of you will also have a small hypodermic injection gun. But we'll talk more about that later."

Sven raised his hand and asked, "Will the pilots have any weapons, sir?"

Asher explained that since the pilots would be posing as civilian U.N. pilots, carrying guns would incite too much suspicion. "But," Asher offered as a caveat, "they will have a couple of Uzis carefully hidden away under the floor of the cockpit. And they'll use them only if the situation goes terribly wrong."

"What could go wrong?" Ty wondered sarcastically. *"Only about five million things."*

Asher then looked at a very large hard-shell equipment case nearby that resembled something a roadie might wheel on stage for a rock concert. It had the U.N. logo on it. He walked over to the seven-foot-long monstrosity and rolled it toward the table. After he punched in the combination on the electronic lock, he lifted the cover. "As you can see, this U.N.-sanctioned case contains the basic equipment that INRC inspectors carry," Asher explained. "Sven has been trained to use these instruments. I'll let him explain them to you."

Sven walked to the open case and removed a smaller case nested inside. He flipped the latches on the smaller case and removed an industrial-grade laptop computer and a foot-long cylinder with wires attached to the laptop. "This is a multi-channel radioactive monitor. It registers the energy emitted by a radioactive source and can pinpoint the exact location of each source of radiation."

Sven replaced the case and pointed to two smaller cases also nested inside the larger case. "One is an alloy detector. It's nickname is ALEX, and it's basically an X-ray fluorescence spectrometer."

Ty chewed on the end of his pen and nodded, as if he understood what Sven had said.

"It generates X-rays to penetrate the material being inspected and compares it to a database of all known materials and alloys," Sven added.

Regan smiled and said, "You had me at spectrometer."

Sven and Solly laughed, and Ty smiled weakly as he bit harder on the pen.

"And this," Sven continued, "contains the environmental monitoring instruments. It measures for traces of radioactivity in the air and water."

"I'll bet you dimes to dollars that there's a false

bottom in that big case," Solly offered.

"Give that man a prize," Sven said as he pushed two inset buttons on the inside of the largest case. The upper section of the hard-shell cover silently pivoted open to reveal a dark chamber and what appeared to be an oxygen mask and tank, along with restraint straps.

"So, as you can see, we have semi-comfortable accommodations for one passenger," Sven explained.

"So how are we going to get Dr. Turan in there?" Ty wanted to know.

"That's the tricky part," Asher interjected. "Solly, will you do the honors?"

Solly removed his headdress to reveal a small injection gun woven into a pocket of the material. Asher explained the social taboo associated with touching an Arab man's head, which would allow Solly to conceal the gun without notice.

"A single 40 milligram dose of ketamine works almost immediately," Sven explained. "It's enough to put someone in a deep sleep without respiratory issues. Another dose can be re-administered if necessary."

"And I suppose Solly will have his satellite phone for communication," Regan added. "Since it is triple encrypted, all conversation should be undetectable by the Iranians."

"That's right," said Asher. "But they do have

sensitive equipment that can pick up when a satellite phone is being used. So the team must utilize it only in an emergency."

Ty shifted in his seat. "Okay, but I still don't understand how we are going to inject the doctor, hog-tie him, and hide him in that case."

"That will require what we call real-time, on-the-ground situational adjustments," Asher replied sternly.

Solly chuckled. "I know what that means. We have to make it up as we go."

"I wouldn't put it quite like that," Asher chided Solly. "But yes, you are going to have to create a situation where you can get Turan alone long enough to inject him and place his body in the case. I told you from the start that this is a dangerous mission. Regan and Ty, there's still time for either of you to back out. Tell me now if you want to step away."

The Americans looked at each and shook their heads.

"Nope," Regan said. "Let's do this thing."

19

EARLY THE NEXT MORNING

11,000 feet above sea level
On approach to Bushehr International
Airport

"Bushehr Approach Control, this is U.N. flight four-three-niner, with you level at one-one-thousand feet with information Echo." The Israeli pilot, speaking in European-accented English, talked pilot lingo to the air traffic controller at Bushehr.

Ty leaned over and explained to Regan that English is the international aviation language used at every controlled airport in the world. "Did you hear what he said, Regan? Pilots and controllers pronounce 9 as 'niner' to distinguish it from the number '5' which can sound like 'nine' over the radio."

"Uh huh," Regan said. Regan pretended to listen to yet another of Ty's longwinded explanations of what seemed to her like monotonous pilot lingo. But her mind was a million miles away.

The Iranian air traffic controller's thick voice crackled in the co-pilot's noise cancelling headphones. "U.N. flight four-three-niner, radar contact. One-three miles northwest of Bushehr Airport. Information Echo is current. Expect vectors for the ILS runway two-niner left. Descend and maintain niner-thousand feet."

The co-pilot pushed his microphone button on the right side of his yoke. "Roger, expect ILS approach runaway two-niner. We're out of one-one-thousand for niner-thousand." He then fingered the keyboard between him and the pilot to enter the information for the approach.

Each pilot watched a high-definition primary flight display on the instrument panel in front of them. It reported altitude, airspeed, engine functions, and the altitude of the aircraft relative to the horizon. Between these two screens was a larger multi-function display where a large map appeared showing the bearings and altitudes for the approach.

The co-pilot keyed his microphone again and said, "Bushehr Approach U.N. flight four-three-niner is level at niner-thousand."

"Roger, U.N. flight four-three-niner. You are cleared for the approach runway two-niner left. Contact Bushehr Tower on one-one-eight point one."

"U.N. flight four-three-niner is cleared for the approach. Tower is one-one-eight point one. Roger. Good day."

The auto-pilot swung them around smoothly to line up on the assigned runway. The rising sun was now behind their backs and the towering mountains north of Bushehr glowed with rose and golden hues. Ty could easily make out dozens of oil tankers in the Persian Gulf. Further south was the shape of a huge aircraft carrier surrounded by support ships. After their pre-landing checklist was complete, the pilot and co-pilot took a moment to breathe a sigh of relief. At least this part of the mission was nearing completion and they would soon be on the ground.

The crew and passengers had arrived in Vienna around 10:00 earlier that evening and had taken time to grab a quick meal while the aircraft was refueling. They were back in the air around midnight, two in the morning in Iran. During the flight, each pilot had taken brief power naps while the other monitored the aircraft's progress. When the co-pilot stepped out of the cockpit for a lavatory break, he was pleased to see the four passengers sleeping soundly. The next 24 hours were going to be one of the longest days of their lives.

The pilot let the autopilot fly them down to about five hundred feet above the threshold of the runway, and then he disengaged the auto pilot. With thrust levers gently reduced, he pulled the yoke toward his chest. There was a gentle screech and bump as they settled onto the runway. The pilot then pulled the thrust levers in reverse thrust configuration, and the aircraft slowed to a safe taxi speed toward a private terminal reserved for VIP arrivals.

As the plane rolled along the runway, the pilot opened the cockpit door. Solly greeted the men and thanked them for the smooth flight.

"I guess you blokes have to start acting like United Nations employees now," he said. "You know what we say U.N. stands for, right? It means 'Understanding Nothing.'" Solly laughed at his own joke.

After parking at gate 9, an Iranian ground crew signaled for them to pull forward until the jet was in position for a jet bridge to be moved into contact with the aircraft. The pilots went through their shut-down checklist, and the co-pilot left his seat to stand at the door of the aircraft and wait for the jet bridge to make contact. When the bridge was in place, the co-pilot heard a knock from the other side of the door, and he twisted the large door handle and swung open the door to the right.

Two heavily-armed Republican Guards stood on either side of the jet way at parade attention, their weapons held diagonally in front of their chest. The four passengers moved toward the aircraft door where they were greeted by a man in his mid-forties dressed in Western attire. Three younger assistants stood next to him. Smoothing the front of his blue blazer, the older man stepped forward toward Solly and greeted him in Arabic.

"Peace be upon you. We welcome you to the Islamic Republic of Iran. My name is Parsa Turan. I am the director of the Iranian Nuclear Agency. And these are my colleagues."

Solly reached out to shake Parsa's hand and said, also in Arabic, "And peace be upon you as well. My name is Nabil Samaar from Bahrain. I bring you greetings on behalf of the United Nations."

Solly introduced Colonel Hansen, a.k.a Sven, then pointed to Ty. "This is Dr. Oscar Williams from Western Canada." Ty reached out his hand and tried his best to hide his Texas drawl. "It's a pleasure to meet you, sir."

Parsa smiled and shook Ty's hand. "Likewise."

To maintain her Kuwaiti cover, Regan drew on the little Arabic she knew and said to Parsa, "Salam alaikum." She desperately hoped he didn't start speaking more Arabic to her, or they would be exposed in a second.

"May we discuss the common language we will use to communicate?" Parsa offered. Everyone quickly agreed all further communication would take place in English for the sake of the guests.

Parsa pointed his hand toward the terminal and said, "Well, that's settled. Shall we proceed? Our van is waiting, and shortly we'll share a meal together."

"Just a moment. Dr. Williams and I need to grab our testing instruments," Sven said. Ty and Sven untied the cargo straps holding the large equipment case in the rear of the plane and rolled it out onto the jet way.

Sven said, "Now we're ready to go. We don't travel light."

"Do you need any help with your case?" Parsa asked.

Sven smiled. "No thanks. I'm used to moving it around. We can handle it."

As the entourage moved into the terminal, Regan breathed a short prayer, *"Lord, thank you for getting us into Iran. Please, just let us leave as well."*

Back onboard the aircraft, the co-pilot removed his satellite phone from a compartment hidden in the forward restroom. He quickly keyed in a number and a voice answered after the sound of encrypted scrambling.

The voice on the other end of the line said in Hebrew, "Yes?"

"We are in Iran and the inspectors have departed the aircraft."

The *Mossad* agent on the phone said, "Excellent. After refueling, stay with the aircraft. You may be required to leave quickly. File your flight plan for Vienna, but leave the departure time open just in case."

"Roger." The co-pilot ended the call and moved back into the cockpit to relay the instructions to the pilot.

20

Jezzine, Southern Lebanon

The sun was setting to the west as darkness slowly settled on the mountaintop Hezbollah compound in Jezzine. Abu Bakr al-Bagahdi ended his cell phone conversation with Ayatollah Mazdaki abruptly.

"Yes, we have received the weapons," al-Bagahdi barked into the phone. "We will deploy them tonight." He walked by faint moonlight to his control center where about fifty soldiers had gathered to await his instructions.

Al-Bagahdi had purchased a warehouse outside Jezzine and erected signage identifying the building as a benign storage facility for Tannourine Mineral Water, a large Lebanese company. But the men working inside weren't storing bottled water. They were planning a brutal attack on their enemies.

The terrorist leader ground his teeth as he thought about how much his ISIS troops had been greatly reduced over the past year. At the peak of their Caliphate, ISIS had generated millions of dollars a month from oil production. They had controlled a combined section of Syria and Iraq that was larger than either nation. But it was that murdering dog of an American president who had released America's military to attack ISIS targets without fear of political ramifications.

Al-Bagahdi's broken mind often wandered back to the details of the event that he believed had turned the tide against ISIS. In 2015 ISIS had captured twenty-one Coptic Christians from Egypt who were doing construction work in Libya. Loyal ISIS soldiers had marched the captives to a lonely beach in Libya and had beheaded them. The beheading was videoed for propaganda purposes. When the video was released to the world, al-Bagahdi recalled how the cowardly media outlets cut the footage before the murders. But millions of people viewed the entire brutal process of beheading that was posted online. ISIS technical experts had doctored the video to make the soldiers appear as giants towering victoriously over the victims.

However, even al-Bagahdi understood that even the doctored video couldn't conceal the truth about how the Christian martyrs had died without fear. Most of them were quoting scriptures from the Bible as they faced certain death. Instead of inciting fear throughout the world, the twenty-one Christians became heroes, especially among the Christ-followers in the Middle East. Their names were honored, along with their widows and children. The beheading had ultimately been a mistake. In the place of each man who died on the beach in Libya, a thousand warriors stepped forward to take up the fight against ISIS. Leaders of the Muslim world condemned the event as heartless, inhumane behavior. As the military attacks against them increased, ISIS recruitment waned.

Al-Bagahdi shook his head, banishing the memory of failure away from his thoughts. This time, he would succeed. He turned to the Hezbollah warriors gathered in the room and yelled, "Allahu Akbar!"

The soldiers raised their weapons, shouting, "Allahu Akbar!"

"Tonight," he told the men, "we will strike a blow against the occupiers of Palestine that they will never forget. Fire will rain down upon the Jew-pigs!" He pointed to the six large wooden crates stacked in the middle of the room. "Our brother and ally, the Supreme Leader of Iran, has bestowed wonderful gifts upon us that we can use to splatter the blood of our enemies."

He motioned to a soldier to unpack one of the

crates. Inside each was a new high-tech weapon never before used against Israel—an unmanned drone designed and developed by Iran. The six unmanned quadcopters arrived loaded with over five kilos of C-4 explosive. They flew by electrically-charged batteries, rendering them virtually silent as they maneuvered just above treetop level to remain invisible to radar.

The Israelis' Iron Dome Defense system had previously detected and successfully destroyed most enemy missiles before they hit their targets inside Israel's border. "But tonight, we are going to go slow and low to attack the occupiers," he told the soldiers. "Once we launch the drones, they will fly to the GPS coordinates that we program into the flight computer. When they reach those coordinates, they'll explode with devastating results. And we will be many miles away when they deliver their payload. The beauty of this weapon is that when it explodes, it destroys any evidence that might connect it to those who launched it."

One of the soldiers spoke up. "And what is our target, sir? Are we attacking an Israeli Defense Force facility?"

The ISIS commander shook his head no. The Israelis had killed many civilians in Beirut and Damascus, so only an eye for an eye would satisfy their thirst for revenge this time. Al-Bagahdi's target that night was Qiryat Shemona, a city forty-eight kilometers south of the terrorist compound. Most of the men knew its significance because it was part of Syria before the "land-grabbing Jews" claimed it after the war in 1967.

At al-Bagahdi's command, more soldiers began unpacking the large drones and carefully attaching the explosive package to each weapon's undercarriage. Twelve men, two for each drone, gingerly carried them outside to the launching area. They were careful to space each weapon a safe distance from the others.

When everything was arranged, al-Bagahdi asked his technician, "Are they ready to launch?"

"Yes, sir," the technician replied. "All six drones have been fully charged. Coordinates for the target have been loaded in. As requested, we will launch each drone in one-minute intervals."

Al-Bagahdi felt hopeful for the first time in several days. "Proceed."

He walked to his private quarters inside the warehouse and punched a number into his burner phone. After four rings, the familiar voice of Ayatollah Mazdaki answered.

Al-Bagahdi growled into the microphone, "We are attacking the Zionists any moment. Your drones are brilliantly designed. After tonight, we will finish our business in Jezzine and go to the rendezvous point in Beirut."

"Allahu Akbar! God is great!" shouted Mazdaki and lavished al-Bagahdi with praise. Al-Bagahdi was the kind of intensely focused warrior he'd been looking for, and he wished he had 1,000 of him to lead more attacks. "Once you are in Beirut, I will have an aircraft waiting to transport you and your top *mujahedeen* to Tehran," Mazdaki said. "Together, we will bring the Zionists to their knees."

Al-Bagahdi said goodbye and pressed his finger to the screen to terminate the call. "Inshallah," he muttered. "If he thinks I am going to become a servant to him, he is in for a rude awakening."

21

Qiryat Shemona
9:00 P.M.

On the night of al-Bagahdi's planned attacks, a Jewish family living in Qiryat Shemona prepared for bedtime. Simon Guttenstein managed the Pizza Hut at the BIG Shopping Mall in the southern part of the city. His was the largest kosher pizza restaurant in Northern Israel. Business was good. He and his wife, Nikki, had moved from Tel Aviv to run the restaurant two years earlier, and Simon soon found he enjoyed the slower pace of life in a town of just 25,000 residents.

Qiryat Shemona is the northernmost city in Israel, located at the top of what is known as "the finger" of the Galilee. This narrow peninsula of territory stretches north toward majestic snow-capped Mount Hermon and is bordered by Lebanon to the west and Syria to the east. The name can also be spelled Kiryat Shmona, which means "the town of eight," in honor of eight Jewish agricultural pioneers who defended their settlement to the death in 1920.

Tel Hai was the first name of this early Jewish agricultural settlement founded in 1916. The pioneers settled in the rich Hula Valley north of the Sea of Galilee. In January 1920, two Tel Hai residents were killed in an Arab invasion against the community. A few days later, hundreds of Arab soldiers attacked again, resulting in the death of six more Jewish pioneers. Among those killed was Joseph Trumpeldor, the young captain of the settlement's military volunteers.

Most residents abandoned Tel Hai, but the battles continued for many months. Finally, under the heroic resistance of the Jews who remained, the Arab attackers retreated. The settlers returned to rebuild their homes and renamed the town Qiryat Shemona to honor the memory of their friends. In the city cemetery, a statue of a roaring lion represents the remarkable strength of those who died while facing a much stronger enemy. Every year on the 11th of Adar, proud residents of Qiryat Shemona gather to commemorate their forefathers' courage.

The proximity of Qiryat Shemona to their enemies continued to make them vulnerable to attack throughout the 20th century. On April 11, 1974, three members of the Popular Front for the

Liberation of Palestine crossed the border from nearby Lebanon and invaded Qiryat Shemona. The gang first entered the town's middle school, hoping to kill students. But because it was Passover, the school was deserted. Undeterred, the attackers next entered a nearby apartment building and killed eighteen of the residents, many of them children. Before they could be brought to justice, the killers blew themselves up just as Israeli soldiers stormed the building. Decades later during the war with Lebanon in 2006, the residents endured hundreds of missile strikes, and twelve Israeli soldiers died in the raids.

Modern residents of Qiryat Shemona have become accustomed to enemy strikes, yet they remain celebrated citizens of Israel because they refuse to abandon one of the most dangerous areas to live in the Middle East. Bomb craters from regular missile attacks dot the city streets. Every main building has access to a bomb shelter where citizens routinely huddle awaiting the all-clear signal. This is their way of life and mode of survival.

The houses of Qiryat Shemona imitate those of the original settlement of Tel Hai, a mix of basalt stone with red-tiled roofs. Simon and Nikki lived in one of these uniquely-styled homes. They were in the bedroom of their nine-year-old son, Daniel, telling him goodnight. The Guttensteins were secular Jews, so bedtime rituals didn't involve any prayers or scriptures. Instead, Simon would usually read a story. Tonight his son had chosen one of the Paddington Bear stories about a bumbling teddy bear abandoned at a London train station who tries to find his way home. Daniel loved these stories about how Paddington makes friends and travels the world. But Nikki noticed her husband was struggling to fight off sleep as he read aloud to his son in Hebrew about Paddington's latest adventure.

Simon was nearing the end of the story when he stopped and turned to Nikki. "Do you hear that?"

"Hear what?" Nikki asked.

"That buzzing sound," Simon replied." It seemed to be coming from outside their son's window.

"I hear it now," Nikki said and moved to the bedroom window to open the blinds. "It looks like there's some kind of drone hovering over our street." They were used to missile fire, but Simon and Nikki had never seen a drone in their neighborhood.

Simon had a sick feeling.

"Close the blinds," he ordered, grabbing his pajama-clad son and jerking him out of bed. "Head to the bomb shelter. Now!"

At that moment, there was a blinding flash, followed by a loud explosion. The stone wall of their home folded inward from the concussive force like a paper cup crumbling in someone's fist. Simon crouched over his son by instinct to try to protect him. But before they could take another step, all three family members were killed instantly by the ensuing fireball that consumed their home.

The house across the street from Simon and Nikki suffered similar damage, killing all eight Jewish family members.

Air raid sirens broadcast an eerie warbling shriek into the night, and panicked residents hurried toward various bomb shelters as five additional massive explosions rained over the city. The sirens continued their warnings for the next ten minutes. Then they grew silent, and the agonizing moans and screams of the injured filled the air.

The next morning, city officials surveyed the damage to find a total of forty-five adults, teenagers, and children had been killed in the unprovoked invasion. Sixty-two others had been injured.

The mayor, Avihay Stern, called the Prime Minister to report the casualties. After the call, Prime Minister Natan Abrams began making plans to travel from Jerusalem to see the ravaged city and lend comfort and consolation to the traumatized residents of Qiryat Shemona.

22

Prime Minister's Office
Knesset
Jerusalem, Israel

Prime Minister Natan Abrams was seated behind his desk, his coat off and his necktie loosened. Ziv Kessler and Asher Hazzan were seated across from him in two wingback chairs.

Abrams ran his fingers through his hair in frustration. "This is a classic example of misdirection," he said, venting to his advisors. "While we were focusing on Iran, they slipped in the backdoor with this surprise attack on Qiryat Shemona. I understand that forty-five Israelis have been killed in this vicious attack."

He turned to Asher and said, "Tell me what you know so far."

Asher consulted his tablet. "And sixty-two others have been injured. Four of them are serious and not expected to survive, so the death toll could rise. Assets on the ground in Qiryat Shemona report that drones flew into the city and then exploded. Apparently, they were piloted in at treetop level to avoid detection by our radar. Once in position, their explosives detonated. Our technicians have determined that large amounts of C-4 explosive were used. At this time, we're not sure of the origin of the drones, but Lebanon is the best bet."

"Do we have any way of determining who did this?" Abrams asked.

Ziv weighed in. "I have been in contact with CIA Director Stephen Baker to see what their satellites picked up." U.S. satellites in geosynchronous orbit regularly flew over Israel and can provide much-needed intel in these situations. "The satellites picked up the heat signatures of the explosions," Ziv explained. "But there didn't appear to be any combustible signature of jet or reciprocating engines with heat signatures before the explosions."

"Can you translate that for me?" Abrams asked.

"There are no heat signatures to trace, which means the drones were probably powered by electricity. But the Americans' surveillance satellites can detect unusual motion for any object over a certain mass. This algorithm allows them to eliminate the motion of smaller objects like birds, but it picks up anything with a mass of over ten kilos. Director Baker told me they are reviewing the satellite images to see if they can isolate these drones."

"Is this the work of Hezbollah?" Abrams demanded of Hazzan. "It sounds a little too sophisticated for them."

"I agree," Hazzan said. "And I'm beginning to see a pattern emerge here. Some of our deep-cover assets in Lebanon have suggested that they believe that Abu Bakr al-Bagahdi has set up a base in Lebanon."

Abrams groaned. "The ISIS maniac who tried to vaporize Jerusalem with a nuclear weapon last year?"

"That's the one," Kessler said. "He has all of his territory and most of his fighters in Syria and Iraq. We know Hezbollah is supported by Iran. So maybe al-Bagahdi is in bed with Ayatollah Mazdaki. I believe if you trace the origin of these drone attacks it will have the fingerprints of Mazdaki all over them."

Abrams nodded, thinking about the flight crew and other four assets they had on the ground in Iran at that moment. "I agree. I just didn't know we were going to be fighting two enemies at one time."

"It's the same enemy in two locations," Hazzan explained. "But as the proverb says, 'Cut off the head of the snake and the body dies.' I think we take care of Mazdaki first, and then al-Bagahdi will be reduced to nothing."

Kessler's smartphone began buzzing. "Just a minute. This is Director Baker, let me take this call."

"Kessler here," he spoke into the phone.

"I see. You're sure of this?"

He paused.

"Thank you, Director Baker. We owe you for this favor."

Kessler disconnected the call. "Good news. The Americans have determined from the satellite imagery that the drones that attacked Qiryat Shemona flew from Jezzine in Southern Lebanon. It's only about forty-eight kilometers away from the city."

"What do we know about Jezzine?" Abrams asked.

Kessler swiped through his notes on his tablet. "Let's see. It is a town of about 3,000 residents. But it's popular with tourists, and every summer about 8,000 people visit." Kesller went on to explain how the city is built on a mountainside cliff with a huge waterfall descending into the valley below. Most of the residents are Maronite Christians who celebrate a festival to the virgin Mary each year.

"It doesn't appear to be a hotbed for Hezbollah activity," Asher concluded.

Asher added, "And that's exactly why Hezbollah has set up a command center there. It's where we would least expect it."

The Prime Minister brought his index finger to his lips, lost in thought. "So... we can't just bomb the city. We've got to find out where the members of Hezbollah are meeting. Any ideas about that?"

"Let's ask the Americans," Kessler offered. "Their satellites can take a picture that can read a license plate of an automobile from three hundred miles up in space. Let's get them to focus on Jezzine and see what they can find."

"That sounds like a plan," Asher said. "Call Director Baker back and ask if they can give us another look at the city. Meanwhile, we have a report from the pilots that they have arrived safely in Iran."

"Even if you don't believe in God, you should start praying that they will be able to accomplish their mission," Abrams said. "Otherwise, we may be facing Armageddon."

Kessler frowned. "If Iran completes their nuclear weapon, it won't be Armageddon. It will be another Masada."

Prime Minister Abrams hung his head, as if praying. He was quiet a long minute and finally looked up. He stared at his advisors with a pained expression before he spoke. "When we were young IDF recruits, you remember that we climbed Masada and vowed that it would never fall again. I don't intend to break this vow."

Then Abrams stood to his feet. "Put our nuclear weapon sites on highest alert," he ordered. "If Iran launches a strike toward us, we will launch our warheads immediately in retaliation."

Asher drew in a slow breath. Kessler looked nauseous and pale. "It may result in mutually assured destruction," Abrams continued. "But if we learned anything from Masada, it is that death with honor is to be preferred over slavery." All three men were thinking one thing: there were no survivors at Masada.

"Yes, sir. It will be done," said Asher. "And may God be with us."

23

Jezzine, Lebanon

Al-Bagahdi watched with mounting pleasure the news reports about the attack in Israel. He and his soldiers stood crowded around a large television in the main room of their control center as Al Jazeera's news anchors showed footage from the devastation at Qiryat Shemona.

A female news anchor from Qatar was reporting a safe distance away from several fires in a neighborhood. "In one of the largest attacks against Israeli citizens in history," she said, "officials are confirming that there have been over forty casualties, and many more injuries. A final count is being delayed until the families can be notified. Witnesses described some kind of air assault last evening around 9:30. Some are reporting they counted six separate explosions."

The soldiers cheered wildly at this news.

The reporter continued, "IDF explosive experts

have reported that the damage doesn't appear to be from missiles. Over the years, residents of this northernmost city of Israel have often been targeted by Syria and Lebanon, although officials from both countries are denying responsibility for these latest attacks. A Lebanese government official, who chose not reveal his name, says the attacks are most likely from the Israeli military. According to this official, the attacks were intended to reach Lebanon, but the Israelis mistakenly targeted their own city."

Al-Bagahdi punched a button on a remote control, and the television screen went blank. He turned to his band of grinning warriors and said, "God is great! We have killed the Jewish infidels!"

The men raised their weapons and shouted back in Arabic, "God is great! God is great!"

Al-Bagahdi motioned for silence. Finally, the men settled down. "I have no doubt that Israel will eventually trace this attack back to us here in Jezzine," he said. "And it won't take them long to retaliate with great force. But we're not just going to wait to be killed, and we're not going to run. We are going to give greater glory to Allah. May he be praised!"

The men looked at each other with questioning expressions as they responded back, "May Allah be praised!" What would they accomplish next?

"That's why I chose this sleepy mountaintop

village for our command center," he explained. "Almost all the residents here are Marionite and Melkite Christians. They practice idolatry with that huge ugly statue of Mary in the city. The men are fat, and the women are lazy because of all the money the tourists spend here. Only a few of the thousand or so old and useless men have weapons, and the ones who do own guns use them only to hunt. There are no policemen in the town. If we can surprise them, we can capture the entire city for our own. With the full support of the Ayatollah Mazdaki, I have chosen this city of pagans to show the world that ISIS has not been eliminated."

Al-Bagahdi pointed to one of the fighters. "I have appointed Muhammed Ziraf as my second-in-command. He has spent time in town collecting intelligence. We have come up with a battle plan to attack the city. And we must be quick about it. We know the Israelis will come for us without delay."

Ziraf unrolled a large map of Jezzine on a table. As the fighters gathered around, he laid out the attack plan. "I have divided the town into four grids. The first grid is here by the cliff where the waterfall cascades into the deep valley below."

The Jezzine waterfall was the fifth tallest in the world. It featured a pedestrian bridge near a precipice, a popular spot for tourists.

"We could attack the citizens with our weapons, but Allah has graciously blessed us with a better way to execute the infidels."

At this, the soldiers issued bloodthirsty cheers. One fighter yelled, "That will save us the expense of ammo!"

"Settle down," their leader said. "If Allah favors our plan, there will be a time to celebrate. We will enter the town and first separate the women and children from the men. Then we will march the men at gunpoint to the bridge where we will push them to their death over the falls. If someone resists or fires a weapon at you, put a bullet in their brain. But from what I've seen of these dogs, they will be too afraid to resist. They might even consider it an honor to die for their pagan goddess. Then we will lock the women and children away in the two church buildings and take command of the entire city."

Ziraf nodded his head in agreement. "And," he began, "we will film the entire scene to broadcast our victory to the world. I'll have a camera mounted on my helmet, and Boshra will use a handheld one. Once we upload the video feed, the world will know that ISIS is still strong. We anticipate thousands of new recruits will volunteer to join our army when they see our domination."

Al-Bagahdi took over from Ziraf and commanded

his men to get up. "On your feet! Form your teams, and load up the trucks! We have no time to waste! The Israelis will strike back soon. We will complete this jihad for the glory of Allah. Take no pity on these infidels. Remember your brothers who were bombed and shot in Syria and Iraq. The Christian armies showed us no mercy."

Once the men cleared out, al-Bagahdi pulled out his phone and pressed a single button. After three rings, Ayatollah Mazdaki answered, "Hello, my son. I've been watching the television reports with great pleasure. Nothing makes me smile like a dead Jew. Tell me you have more good news."

"This was just the opening act. The massacre at Jezzine will be historic," he assured him. The men agreed to talk again after the mission was over. Al-Bagahdi walked outside to find his men waiting in eight nondescript trucks. After climbing in the passenger side of the front truck, he waved his arm out the window to commence driving. "Let's go and fight for the glory of Allah!" he cried, as the convoy started rolling slowly toward the quiet village of Jezzine in the distance.

24

The White House
Situation Room

President David Turner was summoned to the Situation Room early in the morning. CIA Director Stephen Baker and Chief of Staff Tyson Alvarez were huddled together whispering and pointing to a tablet when Turner entered the room. They immediately stood to their feet and said, "Mr. President."

"Stephen, Tyson, good morning. Be seated. Now what's up?"

Baker spoke first. "As you know, our intelligence officers at Quantico are constantly monitoring social media for posts by any individuals or groups with ties to terrorism."

The president nodded. "I knew that, of course. I assumed we had successfully hacked most of those accounts."

Baker took a deep breath and said, "We have,

sir. But they keep creating new accounts faster than we can hack them. In fact, there was a new video posted on YouTube this morning that is particularly disturbing. We were able to contact Google, who owns YouTube, to have the video removed. But we don't know how many times it was viewed. YouTube is the largest platform, but there are dozens of other public platforms where anyone can upload a video. We have our people checking these as we speak."

President Turner turned to Tyson. "And I suppose both of you have watched this video?"

They both nodded.

"And you both believe that the content of the video threatens our national security and that of our allies?"

Baker said, "We do, sir. And we were just discussing whether you should see it or not. If you didn't view the footage, and were asked by the press about it, you could plead plausible deniability."

President Turner folded his hands as he weighed the implications of his choice. Then he decided. "Let me see it."

Tyson said, "Yes, Mr. President." He motioned to one of the military aids to lower the lights and begin the video. The president turned his chair to the right toward the flat screen monitor that covered the upper half of the wall.

The screen filled with jumpy, high definition footage taken from a helmet cam. A soldier was running down a narrow street of a small village. The sound of his boots pounding the pavement pulsated. He was soon accompanied by eight to ten other soldiers who merged in and out of the image. They were dressed in solid black, their faces obscured by a black scarf. Only their eyes could be seen.

Two soldiers carried a metal battering ram, which they used to crush the door handle of an old building. They ran into the building yelling in Arabic. Chaotic sounds of other doors being smashed and shouts could be heard off camera.

The helmet cam rotated to reveal the black-clad soldiers herding dozens of confused villagers who had sought refuge inside the building. They pushed them out of the building and into the street. The villagers did not resist. Soon more soldiers pointing guns at other small bands of men, women, and children joined the mob from other streets. The air filled with crying and indecipherable screaming in Arabic.

The mob soon numbered several hundred of villagers, their attackers forcefully pushing them forward at gunpoint. Above the noise of the chaos, another sound could be heard. It was a deep roar.

The president raised his hand. "Pause it. What's that other sound?"

Tyson whispered, "It's a waterfall sir. We believe the footage is from a small village in Southern Lebanon named Jezzine. It's a mountaintop village built on the edge of a cliff. They have a waterfall that many tourists come to visit."

"I don't like the way this is going. Continue."

The camera panned wide to a pedestrian bridge. The sound of the waterfall was so loud now that it was hard to understand the voices. The helmet cam turned slightly to the right and the scene caused President Turner to gasp in horror.

"Oh my God!" he said.

One-by-one, soldiers pushed the male villagers over the railing of the bridge. The victims screamed for mercy as they fell headlong into the violently churning water below.

Old men who could barely walk were picked up and thrown over as if they were sacks of trash. Some younger men tried to fight but were quickly overpowered and viciously knocked to the ground with the butts of the attackers' weapons. Once on the ground, the invaders laughed and kicked them brutally with their boots before hauling them up and over the bridge railing. Only the youngest boys were spared.

The camera then panned to the left where the women and children had been forced to gather.

Every woman was on her knees praying and wailing in anguish. They were begging the attackers to stop as they made the sign of the cross. The sound on the video was a discordant clash of screaming, praying, and the rush of the waterfall.

When the last man had been tossed to his death, soldiers started marching the women and children back down toward a large church building at the end of the street. Beside the church was a large statue of the Virgin Mary with her hands held out in a welcoming pose. Some of the women in the procession stopped instinctively to kneel and make supplications before the statue. Guards picked them up and shoved them roughly toward the church door. Other soldiers stationed themselves around the building to guard the victims from escaping. The dreadful sound of howling and suffering inside was excruciating. When this church was full, the terrorists would move to the next church in town and fill it with women and children, too.

The camera then panned down the street through which the group from the bridge had been marched. Another mob of villagers appeared. More residents of the small town were screaming and crying in horror as soldiers urged them forward. But they did not head to the church. They were going instead to the waterfall.

Knowing the deadly fate awaiting them, some of

the men produced pistols and started firing at their enemy but were quickly cut down by the automatic weapon fire of the terrorists. Many bystanders were killed instantly by the spread of lethal bullets. The terrified crush of people continued to move closer to the edge of the falls.

The president could hardly bear to look at the screen. "Dear God in Heaven!" he cried. "How long does this torture go on? It's inhuman!"

Director Baker looked at his notes. "The video shows a total of four groups brought to the bridge and disposed of the same way, sir."

President Turner was white-faced with outrage and anger. "I don't want to see any more of it."

"Sir, I think you need to see the last minute of the video. We can cue it to that point," Baker said.

"If you think I must, then go ahead," the president instructed.

The new portion of video was from another camera stabilized on a tripod near a highway about a quarter-mile from the outskirts of Jezzine. The high definition camera zoomed in and there was the horrifying sight of two large churches engulfed in flames. The statue of Mary was lying on its side without the head.

Then the camera zoomed back in and swung smoothly to the left. A warrior wearing black stood still with a long sword drawn from its sheath. The blade was covered in fresh blood.

The man looked into the lens of the camera and spoke in a voice that had been electronically distorted. "Today was a gift for the American president. Mr. Turner, you are no better than goat dung. You thought you had stamped out ISIS? Today is your wake-up call that we are still strong. And with the help of Allah, we will defeat you. We are coming for you and for the Jewish swine who have stolen our people's land." He raised the sword and shouted, "Allahu Akbar!" Behind him the shouts of soldiers could be heard echoing, "Allahu Akbar!"

25

**The White House
Situation Room**

The monitor they were watching went dark. President Turner slammed his fist on the table. "I should have known. This cowardly attack had the fingerprints of al-Bagahdi on it. How many villagers did they murder?"

"The population of Jezzine is about 3,000, mostly Christians," Director Baker said. "We don't know if any residents escaped capture, and we don't think that anyone could survive the fall from the cliff. There won't be a casualty report until the Lebanese officials do their work. And they will not be asking for our help."

President Turner bowed his head for a moment to reflect on the callous murder of potentially 3,000 people. "That's close to the casualty count of Pearl Harbor and the 9/11 attacks." He wondered how the

Lebanese would commemorate the massacre in the years to come.

"This video will be the leading news story on every network around the world, sir," Tyson said. "And don't be surprised when the Muslim press blames this attack on Israel."

"That's exactly what that fox, al-Bagahdi, would want it. Do we have any idea of where he is now?" asked the president.

"No sir," Baker said. "The video was uploaded an hour ago. The time stamp shows it was recorded an hour before that, giving him a two-hour head start."

President Turner stood abruptly. He was livid. "I thought we had him nailed before! Tyson, get me Prime Minister Abrams on the phone. And, Stephen, I know we have eyes over Lebanon. Have your intelligence officers work backward on the surveillance of southern Lebanon to pinpoint any kind of military transport convoy that coincides with this timeline."

Baker pulled out his smartphone and pushed a key. He was soon issuing multiple orders as he walked to the far corner of the room to continue his conversation.

Tyson motioned to one of the aides, who moved to the communications console and entered the data required to initiate a direct audio/video connection with Prime Minister Natan Abrams.

President Turner was pacing around like a caged lion. After less than three minutes the aide said, "Sir, we have a live feed to Jerusalem and the Prime Minister."

Abrams' image appeared on the same monitor where Turner had just witnessed the unthinkable atrocities. The president remained standing to take the call. "Good evening, Mr. Prime Minister. I hope I didn't interrupt your dinner."

Abrams had a somber expression as he said, "No. No dinner tonight. Thank you for calling. I was just preparing to contact you. We are appalled by this vicious slaughter of Lebanese civilians and have sent our condolences to President Berri, but we haven't heard anything back. I'm sure he and other governments will be blaming Israel."

President Turner replied, "Of course. That always happens. We know that you would never do something like this. But that won't stop the United Nations from voting on a resolution to condemn Israel."

"We expect their biased behavior by now. In fact, we keep copies of the resolutions against Israel in our staff bathroom, if you get my drift."

Turner smiled slightly. "I do. That reminds me. Do you have any idea where al-Bagahdi is now? He's like a fox, you know. He strikes and then he flees."

"The Lebanese massacre, coupled with this attack against residents of Qiryat Shemona last night, is the work of the Fox I'm sure. We have forensic evidence that the attack was carried out by four-bladed drones carrying C-4 explosive. Our radar didn't detect them. But your military helped us pinpoint the origin point as just outside Jezzine. We were planning a reconnaissance mission to find the terrorists when al-Bagahdi moved first and murdered the citizens of Jezzine. We're holding him personally responsible for two deadly terrorist attacks within twenty-four hours."

President Turner said, "And he couldn't have done any of that without a lot of help. The CIA is convinced that al-Bagahdi is receiving weapons and soldiers from Mazdaki."

"Our intelligence agrees. This conflict is going to get much more dangerous...soon, I fear. We must consider the ramifications of a declaration of war between Israel and Iran."

"You may be right, my friend," the president offered, taking great care with his words. "But remember, a declaration of war against our allies is a declaration of war against America. There is no greater friend to America than Israel."

Abrams smiled. "Thank you, Mr. President. And we both know which side the old Russian Bear will choose to support."

CIA Director Baker walked over to the president and whispered in his ear. The president turned back toward the video screen. "I had hoped that we would be able to get an eye on al-Bagahdi from one of our birds. They have evidence of a convoy of eight vehicles driving north out of Jezzine. Soon after, smoke can be seen rising from the city. But after about that, the convoy disappeared into Beirut, and we lost visual contact. We have some deep-cover operatives in Beirut. We'll notify them to be on the lookout for the Fox."

"Good idea," said the president. "Tell them to stay away from his sharp teeth. Is there anything else I need to know about in Lebanon or Iran?"

Natan hesitated. "No, that's all for now. I'll keep you posted."

The connection was broken. The president turned to Tyson. "We still have the carrier strike group doing maneuvers in the Persian Gulf?"

"Yes sir, Carrier Strike Group 2 with the USS *George H.W. Bush* is on station in the Persian Gulf," Tyson said.

"Perfect," said President Turner. He wondered why Abrams didn't want to tell him about the covert operation in Iran involving two United States citizens. He vowed he would never leave the Americans behind in a situation that was evolving into what looked like World War III.

26

Bushehr Nuclear Power Plant
Bushehr, Iran

After an hour's ride on bouncy roads, the U.N. inspection team was still several miles away from the Bushehr Nuclear Power Plant. They had eaten a meal with Dr. Turan and his associates, and it was now the middle of the afternoon. Parsa had patiently answered all of the nuclear-related questions from the group. Solly and Sven did most of the talking because they understood the technical nature of nuclear energy. As Regan listened to their conversation, she found herself liking Parsa. He seemed to be a combination of intelligence and kindness, something she hadn't picked up from any of the other members of his team. She thought for a moment how sad it was that they were going to have to kidnap him. Then she shook that feeling off as she remembered that he was willingly building a bomb to destroy Israel.

When the conversation lagged, Regan said, "Dr. Turan, I hope you don't mind my asking a personal question, but have you ever traveled to the United States? Your English is excellent."

"Thank you," Parsa replied. "Yes, I actually spent several years in Texas. I received my Ph.D. in Nuclear Engineering from Texas A&M University."

Ty smiled, "So you're an Aggie. I hear they are crazy about their football team there."

"Yes, I suppose so," Parsa said, a smile crossing his lips. "When I first arrived on campus, I heard the term 'Aggie' but didn't know what it meant, and I was too embarrassed to ask."

Ty explained that the letters "A&M" stand for Agriculture and Military. In 1949 the school named its yearbook Aggieland, and since that time they have been known as the Aggies.

Regan stared at Ty and said through her teeth, "Thank you Dr. Williams, I didn't know Canadians were so well-versed in American college football."

Ty easily batted away her question and replied, "One of my hobbies is American sports trivia. I love it."

"I kept my head pretty much in a book or behind a computer screen," Parsa explained. "I never even attended a game! The Iranian government paid for my education, and I had signed a contract to return to work at the Iranian Nuclear Agency. That's what I've been doing the last ten years."

Ty also felt comfortable talking with Dr. Turan off the record. "Are you married? Do you have family?"

Parsa laughed. "Now I remember. North Americans have a habit of asking personal questions the first time you meet someone. But I don't mind the question." He paused and seemed downcast. "Yes, I have a wife named Esta, but she and our son, Ahmed, are living with her parents in Kuwait now."

Ty had the manners not to dig any deeper on that subject. Just then, Solly pointed forward and said, "I can see the Bushehr security checkpoint just ahead."

As the van pulled up to the gate, the passengers gazed at four enormous smokestacks jutting out of the desert floor, thin tendrils of steam rising into the air. The guard collected all the identity papers of the passengers as Parsa explained in Farsi the purpose of their visit.

The guard handed back the papers and opened the gate. The van drove another ten minutes to reach the parking lot closest to the front entry of the plant. Solly was careful to notice the placement of the anti-aircraft missile batteries and the location of the armed Republican Guard members.

As the group walked through the front door, there were four armed guards holding MPT-9 submachine guns. The commanding officer demanded to see the papers of everyone, including Dr. Parsa and his assistants. Then he took a long time examining the identification documents of the four U.N. inspectors. Finally, he waved them forward to a male and female soldier, each holding metal detecting wands. The female soldier motioned for Regan to step forward into a separate room where she carefully passed the wand over every part of her clothing.

The male soldier instructed Solly to hold out his arms as he meticulously examined his clothing from his shoes to his shoulders. He even waved the wand under Solly's long beard. Solly smiled at him and thought, *"I hope there isn't any metal in the injection gun under my guhtra."* But the soldier avoided his face and head. The wand screeched when he passed it near the walking cane, but seeing the solid gold-encrusted handle, he ignored the warning. Satisfied, the soldier stepped away and waved Ty forward to be searched next.

After Ty and Sven passed the examination, Regan joined them again and Parsa motioned them toward the elevator. Two armed guards accompanied them. Parsa inserted his keycard into a slot, and the elevator door opened. It was a large freight elevator, but after Sven rolled the equipment case in, there was only room for seven passengers.

Parsa spoke to his assistants. "The guards can come with us. I don't need you for the inspection. You can return to your work stations."

Parsa, the two guards, and the four inspectors crowded on one side of the equipment case. He inserted his key card again into the elevator panel above the buttons. He pressed sublevel 2. Solly noticed that they entered on G level and that there were a total of six sublevels on the elevator panel.

"Only sublevel 2, hmmm. I'll bet we won't be invited to inspect what is deeper in this facility," he thought.

27

Sublevel 2
Bushehr Nuclear Power Plant

The elevator doors slid open on sublevel 2. As the inspection team walked out, they entered an observation area just outside what appeared to be a decontamination room. Dr. Turan instructed, "Your technician and I will change into the protective suits for the technical aspects of the inspection. The rest of you can stay in our observation area while we take the readings."

Parsa and Sven went into stalls inside the decontamination room and changed into bright yellow jumpsuits to shield them from radiation. They also donned helmets and thick gloves. Large glass windows separated the observation area from the vast floor space that featured four house-sized structures with metal domes. These were the nuclear reactors where radioactive fuel was placed. Water was pumped into the reactors and heated by the enriched uranium cones. This process produced steam that drove the enormous electric generators. The sound of a deep hum could be heard and felt under their feet.

The two armed guards, along with the three inspectors, remained in the observation area as Parsa and Sven walked into the reactor space. They approached one of the reactors, and Sven unlatched his equipment case and began to remove the necessary instruments for inspection.

Meanwhile, Solly, Ty, and Regan sat on a bench and watched patiently while Parsa and Sven went to each of the four reactors to take readings. The trio kept their conversation professional, but the whole time they were each racking their brains to figure out the best way to accomplish their mission. The two guards remained standing with loaded weapons at their side.

After two hours, Sven had completed the inspection of all four reactors. He and Parsa entered the decontamination area once more where they removed their protective jumpsuits and went around the corner where three private "decon showers" and eyewash stations were featured. Sven returned to the observation room dressed in his U.N. officer uniform. He sat down, opened a handheld digital device, and brought up the data of his readings.

The three observers took some time to examine the information without betraying the fact that none of them understood the readings. Finally, Sven said to Solly, "As you can see Dr. Samar, all the readings are within prescribed levels."

Solly, Ty, and Regan continued to study the screen and make additional comments. They didn't notice Parsa as he walked to the other side of the room and opened the equipment case to repack the instruments for Sven. Out of curiosity, he depressed the two buttons he saw on the side of the case. The false floor of the case flipped up. Parsa looked inside and saw an oxygen tank, mask, and restraints.

Puzzled, Parsa turned to one of the guards and said in Farsi, "Something's wrong here. Come check this out." The guard started across the room toward the case.

Sven understood Farsi and whispered, "We're in trouble," nudging Solly to look in the direction of the open case. Solly and Ty jumped up and walked quickly toward Parsa and the guard.

Solly forced his voice to remain calm and asked, "Dr. Turan, what seems to be the problem?"

Parsa and the guard ignored Solly and both continued examining the case. Before they could react, Solly twisted the handle of his case and removed the knife. He came up behind the guard and wrapped his left arm around the soldier's neck. Solly plunged the knife deep into his back and twisted it up into his heart.

The other guard started to protest in Farsi. In one motion, Ty pushed Solly, the guard, and Parsa to the floor. Ty grabbed the machine gun from the guard as the man fired. A spray of bullets went high, striking the wall above the case. Ty stayed low and rolled to his left, while he flicked off the safety. He fired two short bursts, and the guard fell to the floor before he could fire his weapon again.

The silence was deafening, and the smell of cordite filled the room.

Parsa sat up and yelled, "What's going on?"

He never received an answer because Solly removed the injector gun from his headdress and placed it on Parsa's neck. He depressed the trigger, and the Ketamine flowed quickly into Parsa's bloodstream.

Parsa looked at him blankly and said, "Who are you? And what did ...."

Before he could finish the question, he was unconscious. Sven moved quickly to remove the machine gun from the other dead guard. He glanced around. "There are security cameras aimed at the reactors, but I didn't see any in here. Maybe we caught a break."

"Hurry! I'm sure they heard those gunshots,"

Regan said. "More guards will be here soon."

"We're so far underground, there's no way they heard shots," Solly countered. He removed his satellite phone and looked at the screen. "And that also means I can't get a signal down here. We're on our own, folks."

Sven and Ty carefully lifted Parsa and placed his limp body in the equipment box. Ty pulled the restraints around his arms and legs and removed the keycard from around Parsa's neck. Sven placed the oxygen mask on his face and pulled the elastic band around the scientist's head. Then he opened the valve on the oxygen bottle. Once Parsa was secured, Ty and Sven worked together to replace the instruments and store the two machine guns inside. Then they latched the case shut.

The four of them looked at each other, waiting for someone to speak. Solly calmly wiped off his dagger and replaced it in his cane. He smiled and said, "And we thought our biggest problem would be finding a moment to get Parsa in the case. He took care of that problem for us!"

Ty was not so happy. "That's true, Sol. But that guy almost got us killed, too. If the second guard had been a better shot, none of us would be alive."

"At least now we have a couple of weapons if we need them," Sven offered.

"But guys, what good are two guns when there

are dozens of guards up on the surface?" Regan asked. She was beginning to feel truly terrified. They were outnumbered in a hostile country that would show invaders no mercy.

"Hold on. I've got an idea. It's a long shot, but this just might work to get us out of here alive," Solly said.

28

Sublevel 2

Bushehr Nuclear Power Plant

After hearing Solly's strategy, Ty, Regan, and Sven agreed that it was most likely going to fail. But they were willing to execute it to the best of their ability or die trying. It was early evening now. First, they hid the bodies of the two guards in a supply closet after going through the men's pockets and finding a key fob with Farsi writing on a tag sharing the keyring. Sven translated the scrawl to discover it was an ignition key to a Khodro military equipment truck with a license number. Khodro motors are the largest automotive company in Iran.

"Now, all we need to do is to match the license number, and we'll have our ride out of here." Ty said.

Regan looked at him incredulously. "How many trucks do you think are up there full of guards?" she asked. The boy was cute and she loved him sincerely, but he could be so simple sometimes.

"It's a good plan, Regan," Ty complained.

Sven ignored the squabbling couple and found a Geiger counter in one of the spare rooms. He went to work rewiring it to give a false reading. He fiddled with the mechanism until the counter crackled loudly. Then he turned it off and instructed Regan to carry it.

Solly checked on Parsa, taking his vitals. He was sleeping peacefully. At the agreed upon time, Sven and Ty rolled the equipment case over to the elevators. Solly inserted Parsa's keycard. The doors immediately slid open. Solly took a deep breath, then he inserted the card and pressed "G" for ground floor. As the elevator started to rise, he looked at Ty and Regan and said, "Remember to let Sven do all the talking."

The elevator stopped. As soon as the doors opened, Sven pushed his way out of the elevator and started shouting in Farsi, "Emergency! Emergency! There has been a containment breach!"

Solly and Ty pushed the equipment cart out, followed by Regan who pasted a frightened look on her face. She carried the Geiger counter which was chattering at an alarming rate. Solly paused to push the elevator button for Sublevel 6 before he exited. The doors slid closed as the empty elevator started down.

The guards filling the lobby stood there

temporarily frozen by the news. Sven ran up to the commander and said, "Quickly! There is no time to lose. The breach happened on sublevel 6. We begged Dr. Turan to evacuate with us, but he insisted on trying to mitigate the breach. The guards are still with him. May Allah give them mercy and strength!"

The commander was dumbfounded, and his face had turned white. "This has never happened before. What should we do?"

Sven continued to push the equipment case toward the exit. He yelled in a commanding voice, "Dr. Turan said that you must trigger the warning and enact the evacuation protocol immediately!" Wearing the U.N. officer's uniform only enforced his authority. "Listen to that Geiger counter. It's off the charts. We are all exposed. Quickly, man, tell your troops to leave the facility. Move it, soldiers!"

By the time the team arrived at the exit, the warning klaxon was blaring. Sven handed the key fob to one of the guards. He ordered him to find that vehicle and drive it to the front door. The guard grabbed the fob and sprinted toward the parking lot.

Guards poured out of the building like ants. Dozens jumped into jeeps and transports, heading for the gate at the perimeter fence. A military equipment truck came screeching to a halt in front of the exit of the building. The guard jumped down from the driver's side and ran up to Sven. Sven commanded the guard to help him and Ty secure the equipment case in the back of the truck.

The three of them lifted the case up the cargo area. It was considerably heavier with Parsa's unconscious body inside. Shouting over the eerie blaring of the warning siren, Sven ordered the young and terrified guard to get as far away from the building as possible. The boy turned and ran toward one of the troop transport trucks that was starting to roll out. He jumped in the back, and the other guards pulled him to safety as the truck accelerated toward the gate.

Once he helped Ty tie down the equipment case securely, Sven jumped down from the bed of the truck and ran to the driver's side door. He noted that the building lobby was empty. Everyone had fled, as planned.

Ty, Regan, and Solly had already crowded into the cab space that was designed for three adults.

"Let's go!" Solly shouted, pounding the dashboard with his palm.

Sven swung the truck around and drove toward the exit gate. It was unmanned, so he drove through without slowing down. He could see the taillights ahead of the fleeing vehicles in the distance.

"Where are we going, Solly?" he asked.

"Just keep driving for now. I'm calling the Boss."

Solly fished out his satellite phone and punched in a number he had memorized. After a few seconds, Director Asher Hazzan was on the line. Solly explained the situation. They spoke for another few minutes, and Solly ended the call.

As the sparsely equipped truck bounced over the bumpy highway, nobody spoke for a minute. Regan broke the silence, "So, what's the plan now? Are we going back to the airport?"

Solly shook his head. "Asher is convinced that we wouldn't make it to airport. In fact, he is pulling the pilots out of there as soon as he can figure out a way to do it safely without breaking their cover. He says that when the alarm was activated at Bushehr, it set off warnings at many other places. It won't be long until the Revolutionary Guard troops and Iranian police will return to the plant, and then they'll be looking for us."

Sven was concentrating on missing as many potholes as he could. After swerving again, he asked, "So, what did the director advise us?"

Solly paused. "He told us to hide."

29

Bushehr International Airport
Bushehr, Iran

The Israeli pilots had spent a long day waiting at the airport. After refueling, they had wandered into the terminal to try some of the local food. They weren't impressed with the airport cuisine. They avoided talking to anyone and blended in with the other anonymous pilots and flight crews.

They were seated in the passenger section of the aircraft trying to get some rest when the satellite phone they'd hidden in the restroom began to ping. The co-pilot entered the bathroom and closed the door. He opened the undersink compartment and extracted the phone.

"Yes?"

"Just listen and then acknowledge," an unidentified voice commanded. "Plans have changed. You are in danger of being discovered. Here are your new orders."

The agent continued to give instructions to the Israeli pilot. Finally he said, "Do you understand?"

"Yes, sir. Completely." The co-pilot ended the call and returned the phone to the compartment. He opened the bathroom door and said to his colleague, "Let's go. We're leaving now."

The pilot got up and took his seat in the cockpit. The co-pilot closed the aircraft door to the jet bridge and settled in the right seat in front of the instruments. He quickly explained the plan to the other pilot as he tuned in the frequency for the Automatic Terminal Information System to listen to the latest airport conditions. Then he switched to the ground control frequency and keyed his microphone. In a slow, professional voice he said, "Bushehr Ground, good evening. U.N. flight four-three-niner at Gate 9 with information Sierra. We are ready for immediate pushback. And we'd like to activate our flight plan to Vienna."

The controller said, "Roger, U.N. flight four-three-niner. Sierra is active. Expect push back in five. And flight plan activated to Vienna. Squawk 7431."

The five-minute wait seemed like an eternity to the pilots. Fleeing a hostile threat in an aircraft made them a big target, and it did not help matters to realize their cover could already be blown and guards could be on their way at that moment to take them out. Instead, obliging ground crew members arrived to push the aircraft away from the gate. Once the tug had disconnected, the pilots spooled up both engines.

After a six-minute taxi, they were cleared for takeoff. The EMR-45 jet sailed down the runway and climbed to its initial departure altitude. The next few minutes marked the most critical part of their escape. They still had no idea if or when the Iranians had discovered their ruse.

The pilot said calmly, "Bushehr Departure, good evening. U.N. flight four-three-niner with you at four thousand feet."

"Roger, U.N. flight four-three-niner. Radar contact one-two miles west of the airport. Climb and maintain three-two thousand."

The pilot grinned silently.

"Roger, U.N. flight four-three-niner is out of four thousand for three-two thousand."

The pilot reached over and turned off the transponder, then he deliberately disobeyed these instructions and put the aircraft into a descent until they were two hundred feet above the surface of the Persian Gulf.

While the Iranian controller assumed they were climbing to thirty-two thousand feet and heading toward Vienna, the Israeli pilots had been warned not to fly at high altitude to avoid being targeted by an Iranian missile. Instead, they were now streaking across the Persian Gulf toward Bahrain International Airport.

In an aircraft, a transponder communicates to air traffic control the aircraft's speed, direction, and altitude. Each aircraft is given a different four-digit transponder code, known in shorthand as "squawk." The U.N. aircraft had been instructed to squawk 7431. Since the pilot had turned off the transponder, the Iranian controller could only see a primary radar target limited by obstructions. He would be in contact with the pilot at any moment to see what was wrong.

"U.N. flight four-three-niner. Bushehr Departure. Radar contact is lost. Are you still squawking 7431?"

The pilot responded, "Roger, Bushehr Departure. We have had some trouble with this transponder. It may be erratic or inoperable."

"Roger, U.N. flight four-three-niner. Continue to climb to assigned altitude. Once you leave Iranian airspace, contact Kuwait Approach Control on one-three-three point five."

The pilot nodded, while looking out his window at the surface of the Persian Gulf. He replied, "Roger, Bushehr Departure. We are climbing through one-seven-thousand to three-two thousand. Kuwait approach on one-three-three point five. Good evening. Thanks for the help."

According to their GPS the pilots were on track to arrive at Bahrain in less than thirty minutes. By flying at a low altitude, the Bushehr radar would be unable to track them. Bahrain, a Muslim majority nation, practiced many Western customs. They would be friendly toward a United Nations aircraft. But the pilots would have to come up with a good excuse to land since they hadn't filed a flight plan to Bahrain.

When the GPS showed that they were ten minutes from landing in Bahrain, they climbed to ten thousand feet and switched the transponder to 1200, the appropriate code for flights using VFR (Visual Flight Rules) rather than relying on their instruments. It was time to make contact with Bahrain and see if their cover story worked.

"Bahrain Approach Control. This is United Nations flight four-three-niner. We are forty miles northeast at ten thousand feet. Squawking VFR. We'd like to divert and land there due to some inoperative instruments."

There was a delay of a long few seconds.

Suddenly a voice broke into the silence. "UN flight four-three-niner. Bahrain Approach Control. Squawk 4221. Information Tango is current."

The co-pilot put the provided four-digit code in the transponder and anxiously awaited the next instruction. "Roger, Bahrain Approach," he said to the controller. "Squawking 4221. Information Tango."

"UN flight four-three-niner. Radar contact three-two miles northeast. Descend and maintain four thousand feet. Expect vectors to runway three-zero right."

The pilots looked at each other and breathed a deep sigh of relief. They would be safely on the ground soon. *Mossad* had instructed them to taxi to a private aircraft maintenance hangar where their operatives would tow the aircraft inside. Over the next few days it would be repainted and transformed into a ubiquitous business jet. The two pilots would trade in their U.N. identity to pose as corporate pilots flying to Europe before returning to Israel. They were fortunate, but they had a sickening feeling that their four passengers had not fared as well.

30

Somewhere outside Bushehr, Iran

Sven drove until he passed a deserted house sitting several hundred yards off the highway. He turned the big truck onto the rutted trail toward the dilapidated structure and parked behind the house until the vehicle was hidden from the road. Sven turned off the light and switched off the engine. For a moment, the only sound penetrating the night was the clicking of the engine as it cooled down.

No one had been enthusiastic about hiding until they received further instructions. They were all creatures of action and felt better when they were doing something constructive. But orders were orders.

They climbed down out of the cab and suddenly felt the weight of fatigue that comes after an adrenalin rush. Sven and Ty climbed up into the back of the truck to retrieve the weapons and to check on their cargo.

Sven raised the lid of the concealed chamber and directed his LED flashlight toward Parsa. It seemed as if the researcher hadn't moved. Ty bent down and took Parsa's wrist to check his pulse. It was normal, and he seemed to be breathing well.

The Ketamine dose would keep him unconscious for about an hour, but no more. They would have to administer an additional dose if they needed more time, but Solly had suggested that they allow him to wake up. Parsa might have some important intel that they could leverage to assist them in their escape.

Because there was no longer a need for their disguises, Solly and Regan took turns in the back of the truck changing into attire more suited for their escape. Regan had tossed off the hajib as soon as they left the nuclear facility. When she finished changing into cargo pants and a black tee shirt, she jumped down from the truck and said, "Man, I'm so glad to get out of that long dress and heels. Whoever said that women like wearing high heels should be shot on sight."

After Solly changed clothes, he walked to the edge of the gutted house and glanced down at the highway. What he saw caused his heart to miss a beat. Dozens of headlights in the distance were driving in a line toward them on their way to the Bushehr plant.

Some of the vehicles had flashing lights. Solly knew they were about to lose any element of surprise they had gained.

He whistled softly and motioned for the others to join him. They hid in the dark shadow of the house as military and police vehicles roared past. They counted fifteen vehicles. Soon the night was quiet again, and the four were alone with their thoughts. They all jumped when Solly's phone began to beep.

He punched a button and raised the mouthpiece to his lips and blurted, "You were right! It didn't take them long to figure it out. Fifteen vehicles just passed us heading back to the power plant." He paused to listen.

"According to the GPS on my phone we are twenty-two miles outside the city of Bushehr," Solly continued. "We're about halfway between the city and the power plant. We're hiding behind an old farmhouse."

He listened again.

"Okay. I like that plan. It could work. We're on it."

Regan said, "What's the plan?"

Solly smiled. "I'll give it to the Prime Minister. He can get things done in a hurry."

"Solly, what's the plan?" Regan repeated, betraying fear in her voice.

Solly could see Regan was frightened. "It's simple,"

he said. "We're going to be okay. First, we follow those vehicles back toward the plant."

Ty shot Solly a frustrated look. "Why would we do that?"

"That's what they won't be expecting," Sven interrupted.

"Right," Solly continued. "Then about a mile before the gate, we turn south toward the Persian Gulf. We are going to be rescued by the United States Navy off the USS *George H.W. Bush*. The Prime Minister cleared it with your president, and he issued the order. They have the frequency of my phone, so they can track us in real time."

"What are we waiting on?" Ty yelled. "Let's saddle up!"

Regan smiled at Ty and squeezed his knee. Solly was right. It was going to work out, and they'd all be laughing soon about having had another close call.

Within minutes, they were back on the road heading in the direction of the power plant. A second round of adrenalin coursed through their veins again. Sven drove, and Solly was looking at his phone to call out where to break off the highway and head south.

Sven glanced at his side mirrors and said, "We've got company behind us. A vehicle is gaining on us."

Solly nodded. "Slow down and see if he will pass us."

Sven took his foot of the accelerator, but the car stayed on their back bumper. Suddenly flashing lights painted the night sky. Sven, in characteristically unflappable Scandinavian composure, pulled over to the side of the road. The police car stopped behind them. He saw an Iranian police officer get out and start walking up toward the truck. Sven looked at his companions and said, "Well, let's see what he wants."

Sven opened the door and approached the officer. They began speaking in Farsi. The policeman raised his voice. Sven matched his volume. Soon the first policeman was joined by his partner, and a shouting match ensued. The officers kept pointing at the tag on the back of the truck and shaking their heads at Sven.

Solly nudged Ty, who quietly crawled out the passenger door and knelt near the ground. Carrying a machine gun, he crept slowly down the side of the truck until he was near the back corner of the bed as the arguing continued. When Ty slipped out of the shadows, he saw Sven with his hands lifted above his head. Each officer had drawn their pistols on him.

Ty didn't hesitate. He squeezed the trigger, and the two Iranians twisted to the ground as bullets tore into their bodies. Their firearms discharged recklessly, and Sven dove to the ground to protect himself from their wild shots.

Solly was there in an instant. "Let's load the bodies

in the car. Take their pistols, Sven. Ty, drive the car off the road and try to hide it as best you can. The noise of those shots will carry in the night. I expect we'll have more company soon. We've got to go a different direction."

31

Aboard the USS *George H.W. Bush*
Persian Gulf

The Carrier Strike Group 2 had been ordered into the Persian Gulf by President Turner a few months earlier because of the near-constant threat that Iran represented to the free movement of ships in the region. Iran had threatened to close the Strait of Hormuz, where a third of the world's oil passed through. Strike Group 2 was comprised of the USS *George H.W. Bush*, along with a naval cruiser and three naval destroyers. Attached to the Strike Group were several logistics ships and a supply ship. Roughly 7,500 American sailors and airmen were deployed to this hotbed in the Middle East.

Captain Curtis Morris was in charge of the aircraft carrier. He had flown the F-15 Eagle during Operation Iraqi Freedom, and he had more than a decade of experience commanding submarines and destroyers.

According to regulations, the commanding officer of a U.S. aircraft carrier must satisfy two requirements. He must be an unrestricted line officer, meaning he must have naval combat command experience; and he must be a naval aviator. Captain Curtis Morris was well-qualified on both counts to serve at the helm of the USS *George H.W. Bush*, whose call sign *Avenger* honored the World War II aircraft flown by President George H.W. Bush.

The captain stared out at the night sky from the "island," the command structure poised on top of the flight deck that rose to the height of a twenty-story building above the surface of the water. From this vantage point, Captain Morris and his officers could view operations taking place on the entire four-plus acres of flight deck.

At over one thousand feet in length, the ship was almost as long as the Empire State Building is tall. This self-contained city was home to over 5,000 sailors and airmen. Even at a gross weight of over 100,000 tons, it could split the waves at speeds of more than thirty knots. *"Fast enough to pull a professional water skier,"* Captain Morris had mused when he first assumed command over the vessel. She carried over eighty aircraft, including the F-18 Super Hornet. As he watched the ship lights mirror on top of the Gulf waters, he wondered what this night would hold for him and his crew. He had received an order from President Turner to launch an operation to rescue two Americans and two Israelis who were undercover agents in Iran. He was to also recover their "package," although he had not received the full report of what that entailed. They were now heading full speed for Bushehr on the southwestern coast of Iran. If fired upon, orders were to engage the enemy. Captain Morris had no idea who these agents were, but he was certain they had friends in very high places, considering this order came from the president himself. Typically, this was the kind of call only the Secretary of the Navy issued. However, Captain Morris' role was not to evaluate the order, only to carry it out to perfection.

His officers were tracking a GPS signal from near Bushehr and would soon be close enough to launch three MH-60R Seahawk helicopters off the deck. Each helicopter would be armed with eight Hellfire anti-surface and missiles and GAU-21 .50 caliber guns that fire shells the length of man's hand at a rate of 1,100 rounds per minute.

The United States Armed Forces had never fired weapons in Iran before. At the U.S. Naval Academy, Captain Morris had studied the botched rescue attempt of the fifty-three U.S. hostages in Iran in 1980, and his mind went back in time to recall the details of the catastrophe.

President Jimmy Carter had ordered Operation Eagle Claw, but the Delta Force mission was doomed to fail from the start. Eight helicopters were sent to the first staging area, but only five arrived in operational condition. At that point, it was determined that the mission should be aborted.

However, as the Air Force troops prepared to withdraw, one of the helicopters crashed into a transport aircraft full of jet fuel. The conflagration that followed killed eight U.S. servicemen. The failure of that mission damaged the global prestige of the United States for many years. Captain Morris considered it to be the biggest failure of the U.S. Armed Forces in the twentieth century. Ayatollah Khomeini had used the debacle as a propaganda tool, claiming that God himself had stopped the Americans.

Captain Morris knew there was another crazed Ayatollah in Iran who would love nothing more than to capitalize on another failed U.S. rescue mission. The captain looked again at the radar screen and calculated the distance between his ship and the GPS signal. He picked up his phone and told his Officer of the Deck to launch the aircraft.

Captain Morris watched as the airmen stationed in front of each helicopter circled their hands to indicate the pilots could start their rotors. Even up in the control island, he could hear the sound of the enormous blades beating the air as they were being driven by powerful twin turbo engines. The rhythmic noise increased in intensity as the fixed wing of the rotors approached flying speed.

All three helicopters rose off the deck at the same time and hovered for a moment before the middle helicopter lowered its nose and increased its forward motion. The other two helicopters accelerated, and soon they were speeding across the water toward the coast of Iran.

Captain Morris headed to the War Room where he would follow the real-time progress of the mission. As he joined his other officers, he prayed for his men's safe return after executing a successful mission in one of the most dangerous places on earth for Americans and Israelis to be.

32

Outside Bushehr, Iran

Ty and Sven grabbed the bodies of the two fallen policemen and stuffed them in the back seat of their marked patrol car. Ty climbed into the passenger seat and desperately looked for a switch to turn off the rotating lights pinpointing their position. He twisted every knob on the dashboard before finally killing the lights. He then pulled the police cruiser off the highway and steered it toward an outcropping of rock before jumping out of the car and sprinting back to where his friends were waiting.

Before Ty reached the truck, Solly yelled, "Hurry! We've got company!"

Ty looked down the highway and saw far too many headlights aimed in their direction. As Sven quickly turned the big truck around, Ty jumped into the cab and shouted, "Go! Go! Go!"

Sven stabbed his foot on the accelerator, and the

diesel engine roared in response. For the second time tonight, they were speeding down the same highway, but this time they would meet with certain danger before they got to the rendezvous point with the USS *George H.W. Bush*.

"Any ideas, Solly?" Sven asked. "We've got the whole bunch on our tail."

Solly was already on his satellite phone. "Asher, our cover has been shot. What's the ETA on the cavalry?"

He paused to listen for a few seconds and then ended the call.

"Asher says that the American rescue helicopters have taken off from the carrier in the Gulf. They are tracking my GPS position. We're heading roughly south. He said if there is any way we could travel west, it would shorten the distance between us and the choppers."

Sven was concentrating on the road ahead. Without slowing much, he twisted the steering wheel to the right. As the truck took the turn, it listed dangerously to the right. He shifted down and sped up the unpaved trail. The truck rocked left and right as its tires negotiated the rough road, and Regan reached out instinctively for Ty's arm.

Regan yelled to be heard over the sound of the straining engine, "I hope our passenger in the back is still out. Otherwise he's having a rougher ride than we are!" Regan was thinking she actually wouldn't mind being unconscious right about now.

Sven battled the steering wheel as the truck climbed over the top of a small hill. As he started down the grade, he said, "They're right behind the truck. I don't want them to overtake us. I say we stop here and get our weapons. Let's fight them off and try to buy time until the choppers arrive."

"Do it!" Solly cried.

Sven pulled the truck off the path and turned it around so that the cab faced the crest of the trail. He switched off the lights. The passengers scrambled out and dove for cover under the truck. Sven and Ty raised their machine guns. Solly and Regan clutched two pistols recovered from the policemen.

"How many rounds do you think we have left?" Ty asked.

"Not enough," Solly yelled. "Take your shots carefully."

Several Iranian vehicles reached the top of the hill about fifty yards away. Ty and Sven squeezed off several rounds toward the lead vehicle, shooting out its headlights. The vehicle slid to a sudden stop, and ten or more armed men jumped from the back of the truck and fanned out across the top of the rise and started firing bullets toward the truck. A steady stream of armored vehicles arrived as more soldiers joined the firefight.

As the four huddled together, bullets whizzed past their heads, and some thudded into the ground. Many rounds pinged into the body of the truck. The windshield shattered and then exploded. Solly worried for a moment about the human cargo stowed inside the cab, but he wasn't certain if any of them would survive this onslaught.

Gunfire flashed across the ridge as the soldiers relentlessly fired on the foursome. Ty and Sven returned short bursts toward the Iranians, but they were difficult targets to hit at night.

"How many are out there?" Ty yelled.

"At least fifty. And more are coming!" Sven shouted as he aimed toward one of the men who had just fired his weapon. "That's it. I'm out of ammo."

Solly fired off four shots toward the unceasing line of men. "Listen! Do you guys hear that?"

The gunfire from the Iranians continued, but above the sound of weapons, they heard the unmistakable roar of helicopters arriving behind them. In the next second, the hillside in front of them erupted in flames as a Hellfire missile struck the soldiers' lead vehicle.

The .50 caliber guns from the helicopters spewed bursts of shells that raked across the Iranian frontline. Two vehicles of enemy reinforcements that had just topped the ridge exploded in a fireball.

The four friends crawled out from under the belly of the truck. Two of the choppers hovered over the vehicle and continued to send withering fire toward the Iranian troops. The third aircraft landed a hundred feet behind their position. Before the skids touched the ground, six Marines jumped from the side of the aircraft and started running toward their objective.

"Everyone in the chopper! Now!" they commanded before falling to the ground to provide cover fire. The enemy was undeterred, unleashing a spray of deadly fire toward their position as Solly led his team to safety.

"Are we leaving Dr. Turan?" Sven asked above the fray.

Solly yelled, "He's probably already dead anyway. Nobody could have survived that many bullets."

"No, let's try to get him out alive!" Ty replied.

"Ty! Don't go!" Regan yelled. But he had already turned to make his way back to the truck. Sven joined him. They quickly flung open the door and opened the case, tossing the inspection instruments aside. When they lifted the lid of the hidden compartment, they saw that Parsa was still breathing.

"Let's get him out!" Ty shouted. They untied the restraining straps and pulled on Parsa's body. The deafening sound of the helicopters and gunfire made it hard to communicate.

"We'll have to carry him!" Ty said, motioning toward Solly who was moving Regan toward the chopper. "Help us, Sol!"

Solly instructed Regan to continue making her way to safety. But she insisted on joining him. Solly, Sven, and Ty hastily lowered Parsa's dead weight to the ground. Bullets buzzing around them, Solly and Ty each grabbed one of Parsa's shoulders and Regan grabbed his legs. Sven turned to provide cover for their short sprint toward the chopper as they zigzagged across the firing field. They ran as fast as they could toward the open door of the chopper.

Seconds after they abandoned the truck, a rocket-propelled grenade struck the vehicle. Ty felt the heat of the explosion on his neck. *"Whew! Thirty seconds earlier, and we'd all be dead,"* he thought to himself. He ducked his head, and passed through the line of prostrate Marines who jumped to their feet after Sven ran by, laying down fire as everyone backed their way toward the chopper.

Regan was a few feet from the doorway when Parsa's legs fell out of her grip and splayed on the ground. She looked up and saw Ty had been shot.

She screamed, "Ty! Oh my God!"

Two of the Marines grabbed Parsa and moved him into the chopper. In seconds, they strapped him down on a gurney as another Marine pushed Solly, Sven, and Regan inside.

Two other Marines scooped up Ty's limp body. When everyone was securely on board, half of the Marines jumped out to continue the fight. They would ride back on one of the other aircraft. The chopper lifted off, turned around, and then roared off toward the safety of the aircraft carrier.

33

Over the Persian Gulf

The AH-60R Seahawk's maximum forward speed is 144 knots. And the naval pilot was wringing every inch of speed that he could coax from the twin turbo engines. Behind the pilots, the scene was frantic.

A Navy medic had placed Ty onto his back on a second gurney next to Parsa. Regan had helped the medic cut off Ty's bloodied shirt. She tried not to look at the gaping wound in the center of his chest, blood bubbling out. The medic used his own body weight to apply strong pressure in an attempt to stop the profuse bleeding.

He shoved a manual resuscitation bag into Regan's hands. She knelt at Ty's head. As directed by the medic, she placed the mask over his mouth and nose and pumped the bag with a steady rhythm. Regan was numb with fear and pain. She tried to focus on Ty's face, but her eyes kept wandering back to the medic's crimson-stained gloves covering Ty's chest.

The medic had already added two additional gauze bandages because the blood had saturated the first one. He turned his head and shouted to Solly, "You, sir! Hold direct pressure to this wound. If it soaks through, add another bandage. I've got to get an IV started." Ty was losing fluids at an alarming rate.

Solly moved to Ty's side and used his palms to replace those of the medic, leaning forward to apply maximum pressure to the soaked bandages.

He looked at Regan. He wanted to say it would be okay. But he hesitated. Solly had seen too many men shot. He knew the difference between a gunshot that was fatal and one that wasn't. He didn't want to give her any false hope. Regan was like a daughter to him, and Ty his son.

Regan suddenly raised her eyes to lock on his. Solly could see she was silently begging him to tell her that Ty would survive. Solly looked away, and Regan knew then that Solly believed Ty was gone. There was no hope in his eyes.

She continued to pump the oxygen bag, but she lowered her head and began to sob. She had never known such pain. Her tears spilled from her eyes and fell gently on Ty's forehead.

"I love him. But when was the last I told him?" Regan wondered. *"It was on Masada. How many days ago was*

that? I don't know. We were going to be married. And now he's gone. God, please help me."

The medic checked Ty's pulse repeatedly to no avail. He was gone.

Regan was aware that her hands were cramping from squeezing the bag. She felt a warm hand on her shoulder and she looked up. It was Solly. He then gently placed his other hand on hers, motioning for her to stop pumping.

There were tears in his eyes. She removed the mask and sank back on her knees. Solly had stopped applying pressure to Ty's chest. He leaned toward Regan and enfolded her. Regan desperately clung onto Solly's strong arms. She dissolved into anguish that seemed too big for her heart to contain.

Sven, seated nearby, felt a heaviness in his heart watching Regan suffer. He'd only known Ty a short while, but he was a good man and a strong fighter to the end.

Solly stood up, edged around Ty's lifeless body, and pulled Regan to her feet. As they embraced again, the two of them wept. After a moment, Solly guided Regan to a seat and strapped her in. He sat next to her and draped his arm around her softly, saying nothing for the rest of the journey.

Solly glanced at Parsa lying on the gurney next to Ty and saw that their captive was beginning to wake up from his induced sleep. His dark eyes darted around in confusion as he tried to make sense of the noise and sights around him. The next thing Solly knew, they were slowing down to land on the USS *George H.W. Bush*.

34

The Office of the Supreme Leader
Central Tehran
The Islamic Republic of Iran

Ayatollah Savyid Ali Mazdaki seethed with anger. He was in his office alone with al-Bagahdi, who had dressed for the occasion in the official uniform of a commander of the Iranian Special Forces. Mazdaki had just received a report from the fighting the night before outside Bushehr.

"One of our Revolutionary Guards had the presence of mind to video this attack," Mazdaki said.

Both men studied a computer monitor that displayed a grainy video feed. The rockets and cannon fire was devastating. The fusillade was non-stop as tracers lit up the night like giant, super-powered fireflies. The noise of gunfire and explosions was almost constant. During brief breaks, they could hear shouts and orders from the Iranians. Smoke from burning vehicles filled the air.

"Look," Mazdaki said. "There can be no doubt that those are American helicopters attacking our forces on our homeland. That is a declaration of war."

On the screen, one American chopper rose and accelerated toward the Gulf. Within seconds, two more helicopters followed the first. As the sound of their engines faded, the only audio heard on the video were the groans of agony from wounded and dying Iranian troops.

Al-Bagahdi grimaced. "What a massacre! What was the casualty count?"

"Twenty-six of our soldiers were killed, and thirty-six were wounded. Our commander is certain that our forces killed a large number of the Americans as well."

Al-Bagahdi stood up, feeling emboldened by the embarrassing performance of Mazdaki's troops. If ISIS soldiers had been sent to fight, the outcome would have been much different. "I didn't see any of the Americans shot in this video," he retorted. "This is a disgrace. You must admit you were outsmarted and outgunned. You needed shoulder-mounted rockets. And where were your anti-aircraft batteries? You should have scrambled your fighter jets."

Mazdaki replied with disgust, "So you think you could have made a better plan?" But Mazdaki knew there was a kernel of truth in what al-Bagahdi was saying. It had all happened so fast. There was no intel on the ground near the power plant. Once the enemy had tripped the alarm at the power plant, no one had taken time to report it. Instead, the guards had all left in the confusion.

By now, Mazdaki had discovered that the U.N. nuclear inspectors were frauds. And the head of their Nuclear Energy Agency, Dr. Parsa Turan, was missing.

"Missing?" al-Bagahdi said, laughing. Mazdaki was so incompetent—al-Bagahdi could not understand how such a man had come to power. The Supreme Leader was only useful to al-Bagahdi because of one thing: the nuclear weapons he planned to use on the Jews.

"He's either been kidnapped or killed, according to my sources," Mazdaki shot back.

"Or he may be in on this whole operation," al-Bagahdi taunted.

Again, he was closer to the truth than Mazdaki wanted to admit. Over the last few weeks, he had come to question Parsa's loyalty. But he would never admit this to al-Bagahdi.

"Just days ago, I threatened to execute Turan if he didn't deliver the weapons-grade uranium on time," Mazdaki countered.

Al-Bagahdi sneered. "This smells like an operation

of the filthy Zionists. They are the only ones who could carry out something like this. I only joined you here in Iran because you said you have a nuclear weapon to use against them."

Mazdaki frowned. "We were close, until Turan disappeared. He was the brains behind the uranium enrichment. We'll have to find someone to replace him. But I believe we have another option. I've spoken to the Russian president. I'm convinced that he will supply us with all the nuclear weapons we will need to annihilate the Jews."

"Don't trust the dirty Russians," al-Bagahdi spat. "Their jets killed my ISIS brothers in Syria and Iraq. Don't you remember how they bombed hundreds of our camps? The Russians will turn against you, I assure you."

"Perhaps. But I'll make it appear that I trust them until they deliver the weapon. Besides, they are the only ones buying our oil." Mazdaki paused. "So what is your counsel for our next step?" He hated asking for this fox's advice, but al-Bagahdi was a brilliant military strategist.

"The easiest way to gain the propaganda edge is to release this video to the world. There will be global outrage when other nations see this unprovoked invasion by the Americans. And inflate the body count. They can't verify it. I can have my marketing director edit the video to make it appear as if your men shot down an American helicopter and killed many of the Americans. The fight won't appear as a one-sided massacre that way. Then we will upload the doctored video on all the social media platforms. Just give me the word and it's done."

Mazdaki smiled. "I like the way you think."

"Thank you, Your Excellency," al-Bagahdi said and bowed thoughtfully. Mazdaki wouldn't like the way al-Bagahdi was thinking when he took over one day as Supreme Leader. It was just a matter of time, the terrorist told himself.

After al-Bagahdi departed, Mazdaki pulled out his cellphone and pushed an icon on the screen.

"The Fox is clueless," Mazdaki began. "We have him just where we want him. I've convinced him that he's my trusted advisor. Have your team shadow him. I want to know everywhere al-Bagahdi goes and what he does. If he sneezes or has a cup of coffee, let me know about it. Continue with my previous plans for him."

35

Aboard the USS *George H.W. Bush*
Persian Gulf

Once the AH-60 Seahawk settled onto the deck, crewmen rushed to secure the helicopter. When the blades stopped spinning, the medic slid open the chopper door to let the passengers out.

Regan saw a naval officer standing in the doorway, his hand extended to her. Regan stood, and Solly and Sven each took an arm and helped her out of the chopper.

"Ms. Hart, I'm Commander Curtis Morris."

Regan shook his hand weakly.

"Welcome to the USS *George H.W. Bush*, I'm sorry for your loss, ma'am. I know Mr. Kensington was a decorated Marine pilot. We will treat his remains with the utmost respect and honor."

Captain Morris turned to include Sven and Solly, who had also exited the chopper. "We'd like for the three of you to follow me to the ship's hospital where medics are waiting to examine you."

He motioned toward Dr. Turan, who was being lifted off the chopper on the gurney. "Our crew will attend to the other passenger in need of care," Captain Morris said.

He directed them to an elevator, and they rode down to the ship's hospital, one level below the flight deck. Three naval corpsmen were waiting for them. A female medic escorted Regan into an examination room. Solly and Sven were led into adjoining rooms.

Twenty minutes later, they had all been pronounced fit. Regan told the medic what had happened to Ty, and just talking about it seemed to ease a little of the pain.

They walked into a nearby waiting room and were surprised to see Parsa Turan awake and drinking a glass of orange juice. A medic had a blood pressure cuff around his arm checking his vitals. An armed Marine guard was standing beside him. Parsa looked up and registered a look of confused surprise when he saw the three standing before him.

As his memory slowly returned, he looked at Solly and stammered, "Who are you?"

Solly pulled one of the waiting room chairs across the room and sat down in front of Parsa. "I'm sorry, Dr. Turan. I can't tell you now who I am and who sent us. But I can tell you that we were sent to kidnap you because of your role in creating a nuclear weapon for Iran. Our leaders were convinced that removing you from Iran would delay the process. We mean you no harm. We never meant to incur casualties on this mission, but unfortunately many people died." Solly looked down and added, "Including the fourth member of our team."

Parsa looked around, noticing for the first time that Ty was missing. He took another sip of his orange juice and tried to process all this information. He regarded his surroundings and concluded he was on a ship, most likely somewhere in the Persian Gulf.

"From the look of this guard standing near me, I'm going to guess this is an American ship. Am I right, so far?"

Solly nodded.

Parsa was silent for a few more minutes, taking several sips from the orange juice until he finished it. He carefully placed it on the table beside his chair. He appeared to be battling what to say.

Parsa looked at Solly and confessed, "To be totally honest, I feel safe for the first time in many weeks."

Solly ventured, "What do you mean?"

"I can't say anything until I am certain I am in American custody." He pointed at Sven and said, "You don't look like an American. Are you?"

Sven said, "I'm not. But Regan is an American. And so is your guard."

Tursa noted Regan's eyes were red from crying. "He's right. I'm from Georgia. Ty was the fourth member of our group from Texas. He was shot while we were trying to save you. We were engaged to be married."

"I'm sorry for your loss," Parsa said. He looked at the guard, "Are you an American?"

The Marine nodded. "Yes, sir. I'm from Alabama. It doesn't get any more American than that."

Parsa closed his eyes to think. Regan noticed that his lips were moving, almost as if he was praying. He finally opened his eyes. "Talking about this in Iran would be my death sentence. So, you understand why I'm reluctant."

Solly responded, "Go ahead, Parsa."

The use of his first name seemed to convince him to speak his mind to these strangers. "The Ayatollah had commanded me to create a nuclear weapon," Parsa began. "I have been working on it for the past three years. We have a secret facility six levels down at Bushehr where you came for your weapons inspection. I had complete control of the work conducted there. But I decided weeks ago that I would stop enriching the uranium and, if necessary, even sabotage the operation. I couldn't build a bomb. I believe Ayatollah Mazdaki suspected something was wrong. He gave me an ultimatum and threated me with death if I didn't meet his deadline."

"I don't understand," Solly interrupted. "What exactly made you decide to stop building the bomb?"

Parsa hesitated. Then when he started, his words gushed out. "This past year I renounced Islam and became a secret follower of Jesus Christ. I kept having dreams about Jesus. My wife was having the same dreams. My brother was a Christian and I didn't even know it. Since I started following Jesus, I've been reading the New Testament. Jesus tells us to love our enemies and do good to those who mistreat you. I decided I would not use my knowledge of nuclear energy to kill people. So I sent my wife and son to live with her parents in Kuwait where she would be safe from the reach of the Iranians."

Regan, Sven, and Solly sat speechless as Parsa revealed his incredible story.

Parsa continued, "My religion taught me to hate the Jews. I was prepared to annihilate the entire race. But when I trusted Jesus, I learned that Jesus was also a Jew. Only when I saw the truth about Jesus did I understand the truth about Islam." Parsa went on to explain how he had already slowed down the centrifuges and was going to cause the enrichment to fail, despite Mazdaki's death threat. "So, in a way," he concluded, "it seems that you have saved my life. God answered my prayer for deliverance."

He looked at Solly, "When you injected me with that drug, I thought it would kill me. And my last thought before I lost consciousness was that I would wake up in Heaven in the presence of Jesus."

Immediately, Regan's eyes filled with tears again when she heard these words. What had been Ty's last thought before he died?

She suddenly remembered what Ty had told her when they were standing together on top of Masada before all this had happened. In her mind she could visualize the scene again. The sun had just risen over the majestic Dead Sea. Ty was talking about Leah, a Jewish girl who had also converted to Christianity. She replayed Ty's words to her, *"Regan, I've been meaning to tell you something. The other night in the hotel room...when Leah was praying her prayer to accept Christ...something happened. I felt a huge weight on my chest, and I had to fight to hold back tears. I realized then that I also wanted what it is that I've seen in you. So that night I finally placed my faith in Jesus. I was praying when Leah left the room. Ever since that night I've been thinking about my life from a different perspective."*

Regan looked across the room at Parsa, and her heart felt a mixture of sadness, joy, and hope. *"Thank you, Parsa, for reminding me just where Ty is right now,"* she said in her heart.

36

Office of the Iranian Special Forces
Tehran, Iran

Al-Bagahdi sat at the head of the polished conference table. His closest aides who had fought with him in Syria, Iraq, and Lebanon were seated around him. Since escaping Lebanon two weeks earlier, they had been inserted as a special unit within the Iranian Special Forces. But they still hadn't received any meaningful assignments.

Al-Bagahdi slammed his fist on the table. "Mazdaki is a fool!" Heads nodded in agreement. As planned, al-Bagahdi's men had uploaded the edited video of the American invasion for the world to see. Then Mazdaki held a press conference where he added such inflated claims of Iranian and American casualties that it became evident the video was a fake. This caused outrage in every Muslim majority country. Satellite surveillance quickly proved Mazdaki to be a liar, and he instantly lost credibility on the world stage. Leaders from across the globe condemned Iran for manipulating the situation to their advantage. As a result, Iran had been heavily sanctioned.

Al-Bagahdi continued his tirade. "We have seen hundreds of military victories over the past five years. We've spilled the blood of thousands of infidels. Allah has blessed our efforts. But this madman is going to get us all killed."

It was true. Mazdaki had never appeared weaker, and the Iranians blamed him for the new round of sanctions leveled at their country.

"Now is the time to act!" al-Bagahdi shouted.

His commander waited for his boss to pause before stating, "We agree, sir. Tell us what to do, and we will obey you to the death."

Al-Bagahdi steepled his fingers under his bearded chin, concentrating for several minutes. Finally he looked up. "We need to infiltrate the other units of the Iranian Special Forces. They know about our military successes and admire our courage. We must ruin Mazdaki while his leadership is in question and find out who is willing to support us in a military coup against the Ayatollah."

"Are you really going to try to depose him?" one of his lieutenants asked.

The fire of fanaticism filled al-Bagahdi's eyes. "No.

We're going to kill him and make it appear as if the Zionists have assassinated him. We know they have infiltrated the country already. Then we can launch a full-scale attack against the Jewish occupiers of Palestine. When the Americans come to their aid, we will wipe them out as well."

"But do you have access to nuclear weapons?" another leader asked.

"Not yet, but Mazdaki has negotiated a deal with the Russians to smuggle nuclear weapons into the country. We need to let him live long enough to secure those weapons. As you know, Mazdaki wants a war with Israel to usher in the return of the Twelfth Imam. What he doesn't know is that I am the Twelfth Imam, and Allah has gifted me to establish the Twelfth Caliph!"

At this, the men around the table stood to attention and saluted al-Bagahdi. "Allahu Akbar!" they shouted.

They talked thirty minutes more about their strategy. Each soldier was assigned the name of an officer in the Special Forces to contact about plans for a coup. They would meet again in two days and give an update.

After the meeting adjourned, al-Bagahdi walked out into the oppressive heat of Tehran. His Mercedes S-class sedan was waiting for him in his private parking spot. He unlocked the car, climbed into the driver's seat, and settled into the rich leather upholstery. When he pushed the engine start button, the ignition caught for a split second. A huge explosion split the air as a blazing fireball consumed the Mercedes. Al-Bagahdi was incinerated before he could attempt to escape.

Across the street, an unidentified VAJA agent raised his cellphone to his cheek. "It is done. Al-Bagahdi won't bother you or anyone else ever again."

On the other end of the call, Ayatollah Savyid Ali Mazdaki smiled and said, "Good job. Finally, someone has outfoxed the Fox."

Epilogue

TEN MONTHS LATER

Masada, Israel

Regan led Sven and Solly up the Snake Trail at Masada as the rising sun painted the mountains with bold brushstrokes of changing colors. She leaned into her hiking stick and noticed a thin trickle of sweat slowly dripping down her spine. She smiled. After Ty died, she thought she'd never smile again. It hurt, but she was learning that God provided His peace just when she needed it.

She stopped walking and turned around. Sven and Solly were two switchbacks down from her. "Come on, you guys! You aren't going to let a girl beat you to the top, are you?" She turned and continued to climb.

In less than a minute, Sven passed her as he ran effortlessly up the slope as if it wasn't even there.

"He's amazing," Regan found herself thinking about this Swedish mystery man who had shown

up in her life. As she plodded along, she reviewed
everything that had happened since the night Ty
had died. Everyone predicted that war would break
out between Iran and Israel, but the turmoil had
eventually settled without altercation. Only the three
of them knew that disaster had been avoided primarily
because of how their secret mission had unfolded.

After a few weeks of a tense standoff between
the U.S. and Israel against Iran, the Ayatollah blinked
first and withdrew his threat of nuclear war. Israel
then produced evidence confirming that the drones
involved in the attack on Qiryat Shemona were indeed
manufactured in Iran. Lebanon was quick to distance
themselves from the attacks on Qiryat Shemona and
Jezzine, blaming the deceased ISIS leader al-Bagahdi
for the slaughter.

Some members of the U.S. Congress had
grumbled about what they perceived as unprovoked
military action in Iran and threatened to start
impeachment hearings against President Turner. But
once they got their face time and sound bites in on all
the major news channels, they made a hasty retreat
from impeachment after hearing Dr. Parsa Turan's
testimony before a congressional hearing.

Parsa's information became the turning point in
the entire global crisis. He cooperated fully with the
CIA and during the hearings revealed how Ayatollah

Mazdaki had knowingly broken the sanctions against building uranium for nuclear weapons. Parsa produced digital records proving that the Supreme Leader had ordered him to increase the enrichment of uranium to produce weapons-grade material.

Parsa's face was on the front of every newspaper for days. The CIA had safely extracted his wife and son from Kuwait, and they had been reunited in Washington. Texas A&M had even offered a professorship to their alumnus.

Regan returned to the United States for Ty's memorial held in Tyler, Texas. She was accompanied by Solly and Sven. The worship center at a large church in town had been nearly full for the service. The pastor spoke about how Ty had laid down his life for his friends. He read a statement Regan wrote about Ty's recent conversion to Christ. Ty was laid to rest in the Cathedral in the Pines cemetery with full military honors, including a twenty-one gun salute. Captain Curtis Morris had arranged for the U.S. Navy Blue Angels to fly over the cemetery. Everyone looked up at the roar of the jets above them and watched as a single jet pulled left and climbed into the sky in "missing man" formation.

As one member of the honor guard played Taps, two other officers carefully folded the American flag into a perfect triangle with only the blue and white showing. The officer turned to Ty's parents, Ted and Annette Kensington. He bent down to hand the flag to Annette, but she stopped him and whispered something in his ear.

He stood and took a step to the side to pause in front of Regan. There he knelt down and handed her flag. "On behalf of the President of the United States, the United States Marine Corps, and a grateful nation, please accept this flag as a symbol of our appreciation for your loved one's honorable and faithful service," he told her.

***

Regan had spent a month back home in Georgia wondering what to do with her life. Everything there represented her past. Every time she walked out the front door of her condo, she was reminded of the first morning when she had met Ty.

Regan decided that she didn't want to spend the rest of her days just helping people make money in a global economy. She sensed that God was leading her to help more people like Parsa learn the truth about Jesus. She bought a ticket, flew to Israel, and had spent the last few months assisting Solly in his day job—hosting archeological tours around Israel. She had come to love every part of the Land of Miracles. To her surprise, time had done what it was supposed to do and slowly eased her grief. The pain from losing Ty was not as sharp as before. But her eyes could unpredictably fill up with tears if she heard a song they had liked or if a random memory flooded her mind.

When she wasn't working, she spent a lot of time with Solly and Sven. The three felt relaxed together and could laugh a lot, but they were comfortable talking about more serious topics, too. Solly had become a mentor of sorts to Sven.

As she approached the top of Masada she saw Sven standing there with his arms outstretched, the victor. Sven was handsome, sporty, and brilliant—the perfect guy, really, except for one thing. He had indicated to Regan on more than one occasion that he had no interest in God or the Bible. But that was about to change.

Regan walked up to the Swede, pulled his arms down, and said, "Ha! I let you win, buddy. I knew that your fragile ego couldn't live with a girl beating you, so I took pity on you."

"Give me a little more time with this guy, and he'll be reading the Bible and trusting the Lord," Regan thought. Ty had been much the same way when it came to faith when they first met. He was a natural born skeptic, but she had eventually convinced him to read the Bible for himself, starting in the Book of John in the New Testament. Ty agreed, but only if she agreed they

would talk about all the "mistakes" he found. Instead, Ty had accepted Christ.

"Hey, Sven. I've got a proposal for you," Regan said.

"You're going to have to wait for me to ask you someday, Regan," Sven teased. "No, seriously. What is it?"

Regan smiled at his attempt at flirting. "You've told me several times that the Bible is full of mistakes."

Sven looked surprised at this turn in the conversation. But he replied, "Yes, I think it has obvious errors."

"Well, I propose that you read the Gospel according to John. Then you and I will sit down, and I want you to show me all the mistakes. Will you do that?"

"Sure, Regan." Sven was thinking he would do just about anything to spend more time with this beautiful woman.

Solly arrived at that moment. "What are you two talking so seriously about?" he wanted to know.

"Oh, I challenged Sven to read the Book of John in the New Testament and show me all the mistakes," said Regan proudly. "And he accepted my proposal."

A big grin broke out on Solly's face as he thought to himself how Sven didn't stand a chance. He was a goner for sure.

AUTHOR NOTES

The Masada Proposal is the third book of a trilogy that includes *The Cloud Strike Prophecy* and *The Jerusalem Protocol*. If you enjoyed *The Masada Proposal*, and haven't yet read the earlier two books in the series, I encourage you to do so.

As many of my friends know, the character of Solly is loosely based on my long-time friend and Israeli Tour Guide, Reuven Solomon. He is one of the most intelligent men I know regarding the history of Israel and the Bible. I appreciate his good-hearted willingness to allow me to continue to make him a hero in my books. So, if you ever meet Reuven in person, don't ask him if he really works for *Mossad*!

Although this is a work of pure fiction, there are many factual details in the plot. Iran does embrace the Twelver belief in Islamic eschatology and is committed to eliminating Israel. They even continue to deny the reality of the Holocaust. As I was writing this novel, Iran conducted drone attacks on oil facilities in Saudi Arabia, causing extensive damage. While all of us are praying for peace in the Middle East, many experts believe there will be a significant future confrontation between Iran and Israel.

It is a confirmed fact that many Muslims, like the characters in my book, are coming to faith in Christ throughout the world today. More Muslims have come to Christ in the last twenty years than in the previous fourteen hundred years. My friend, Tom Doyle, has written an excellent book about this trend. I encourage you to read *Dreams and Visions: Is Jesus Awakening the Muslim World?* and then share it with a friend.

The information about the formulation of the Quran and the Hadith is factual, and all quotations are authentic and can be confirmed by consulting either source. The origin of the conflict between Sunni and Shia Muslims is historically accurate as well.

As always, I'm thankful for the Green Acres family who gives me the encourage and resources to travel, train others, and to write. I'm thankful also to Fluency, Inc. for their excellent work in helping publish my books.

Bill and Sharon McKenzie have always been gracious in allowing me a place to write at their

Hilltop Retreat. Bill graduated to Heaven while I was writing this novel, so I am happy to dedicate this book in memory of his friendship.

October 2019
David Orlo
Tyler, Texas

Made in the USA
Coppell, TX
26 November 2019